My Summer of Pink & Green

My Summer of

LISA GREENWALD

Pink & Green

AMULET BOOKS
NEW YORK

Cataloging-in-Publication Data has been applied for and may be obtained from
the Library of Congress.

ISBN: 978-1-4197-0413-0

Text copyright © 2013 Lisa Greenwald
Photography copyright © 2013 Jonathan Beckerman
Book design by Chad W. Beckerman

Printed and bound in U.S.A. 10 9 8 7 6 5 4 3 2 1

Amulet Books are available at special discounts when purchased in quantity for premiums and
promotions as well as fundraising or educational use. Special editions can also be created to
specification. For details, contact specialsales@abramsbooks.com or the address below.

THE ART OF BOOKS SINCE 1949
115 West 18th Street
New York, NY 10011
www.abramsbooks.com

For my brothers David and Max Greenwald, who make everything better just by being there

Lucy's tip for a great summer:
Appreciate every moment.
Summer is fleeting and goes by fast!

School got out a week ago, but it doesn't feel like summer yet. It will soon, though. As soon as Claudia drives up and gets out of the car and runs to hug me, then it will feel like summer. The best feeling in the whole, entire world.

"It's gonna be a Jetta," Yamir says. "College kids always drive Jettas." We're sitting on my front porch drinking my mom's famous homemade mint iced tea: me; my best friend, Sunny Ramal; her brother, Yamir; and our friend Evan. He's pretty much Sunny's boyfriend, but we're all friends with him too. The others always turn their noses up at the mint iced tea, but once it's in the special tall glasses with little pieces of mint floating on the top, they can't resist. It's just too refreshing.

"I don't think so; Jettas are fancy, aren't they?" I ask. We're guessing cars because Claudia's driving home with a friend from school. If Claudia were flying home from Chicago, we'd pick her up at the airport and I'd even make one of those name signs that professional drivers use. But she got a ride home instead. Mom and Grandma were all worried about the long drive, and they insisted that she stop and stay overnight somewhere. Her friend Lauren is the one driving her; she lives in Fairfield, which is like an hour from here.

"It's gonna be some old car," Sunny says, standing up. She wants to be the first one to see Claudia coming, but I don't see how that's going to happen if we don't even know what car she's coming in.

"No way," I add. "Girls named Lauren don't have beat-up old cars. Maybe a Honda, but a new one."

"Maybe it's a motorcycle!" Evan shouts. "Wouldn't that be hilarious?"

I give him a stare-down. "No, Evan Mass, it would not be hilarious, because my mom and grandma would probably pass out from shock. Then we'd have to take them to the hospital." I keep up my stare-down. If he's going to be my best friend's boyfriend, then he can't say dumb things like that. "Motorcycles are really dangerous, you know."

He cracks up, and Sunny and Yamir do too.

I don't see what's so funny. "They are. I'm serious."

Sunny pats my knee. "He was just kidding, Lucy."

Thankfully my mom comes out with a tray holding a full pitcher of more mint iced tea and a bowl of strawberries and breaks the tension. "Hungry?" she asks. When none of us answer, she says, "You know, you guys can go swimming. I'm sure Claudia will come on back when she gets here."

The pool! OK, I changed my mind. It will really feel like summer when we're all in the pool. Claudia will probably run inside and throw on her favorite red-and-white gingham bikini and then she'll race out to join us. We'll have diving contests and make Sunny be the judge. She always gives me a ten. And we'll go down the spiral slide a billion times. Sometimes I even sit on Claudia's lap when we go down the spiral slide. It makes Grandma nervous, but we do it anyway.

Claudia's friends will come over and BBQ like crazy— Grandma always lets them use the grill even though she says I'm not old enough. They'll make hamburgers and hot dogs, and portobello burgers for their vegetarian friends. They'll hang out for hours, and they'll let me hang out with them too, some of the time.

It will feel like summer will last forever, and I'll keep telling myself that it won't last forever but that I need to appreciate it and savor every second: every sip of Mom's iced tea, every trip down the spiral slide, every diving contest.

"She's here!" I scream. I know it's her because the windows are rolled down and her head is out the front passenger side like she's a golden retriever.

They pull into the driveway.

"A Subaru!" Yamir says. "We should have known. College kids always drive Subarus."

I don't even care to discuss with him about how he knows that. I'm too excited to see Claudia, to give her hugs, to talk to her about everything—especially the opening of the spa—that I just don't have time to deal with Yamir.

He's been so weird lately. He doesn't get why it's such a big deal that Claudia's coming home. He takes it for granted that his sister is home all the time, but I haven't seen Claudia since September, since she didn't come home for Thanksgiving. Then she was in El Salvador over winter break, and she went to Ghana for spring break. For an eighteen-year-old, she travels a lot.

I run over to the car and Claudia hops out and we hug for a million years like I thought we would. "I missed you so much," I whisper in her ear.

"I missed you too, Luce!"

Her friend Lauren starts unloading the trunk and I'm thankful that Yamir goes over to help. He can be a gentleman sometimes, but then other times he can act like a complete doofus. Grandma says that's just how boys his age act. But I don't really believe her—can't he just act nicer? For me?

"These are yours, right, Claud?" Lauren asks her, holding up a duffel. Claudia looks over, and that's when I notice that there's another person here. A tall, skinny guy, standing right near the car talking to Evan about the Subaru's muffler or something.

"Yeah, those are mine. Bean's are the ones in the backseat."

"Bean is here?" I ask without thinking.

Claudia does a head-jerk motion in his direction, trying to get his attention, and he comes over to where we're standing. I look around for Mom and Grandma. The moment we've all been waiting for—Claudia coming home—is finally here!

"You must be Lucy," this Bean guy says, with a hand up to high-five me.

"I am." I smile and high-five him back. "And you must be Bean? Well, duh, I mean I know you're Bean, Claudia just said that. But I remember your name. Claudia said you helped look over the grant application a few months ago."

"I did. I did." He nods like he's so proud of himself. "I'm pre-law."

"Huh?"

"It means he's going to be a lawyer, Lucy," Claudia explains.

I feel stupid. I could have figured that out.

"But it's a dual major with the business school," Bean adds.

I nod. Bean sounds like he's on a job interview. I'm not really concerned with his major right now. It's summer! He shouldn't be thinking about school anyway.

"Welcome home!" Mom yells, running outside, a dish towel over her right shoulder. "Ma, Claudia's home!" she yells back into the house.

A few seconds later, Grandma comes out, and then we're all together. I don't even realize that Sunny, Yamir, and Evan went back onto the porch until I hear the click of Yamir's iPhone camera taking a picture of all of us standing around in the driveway.

"Such a photo op," he says with a grin. "Right, Luce-Juice? You're all about the photo ops, especially one like this."

Sometimes I feel like Yamir knows the right thing to do and he does it, but then he says something obnoxious while doing it, and that takes all the goodness out of it.

"Thanks." I put my hand on my hip and go into a model pose and he snaps another shot.

"So, Mom, Grandma," Claudia starts. "This is my friend Lauren, and this is Bean."

I wonder why Claudia doesn't refer to Bean as her friend.

"Lovely to meet you, thank you for driving her home, Lauren," Grandma says. "You probably want to get going. I bet your parents are worried sick about you doing so much driving and all the crazies on the road."

"Grams, it's OK." Claudia pats her shoulder. "She's meeting them nearby, and then they're going to their beach house in Newport for the summer."

"That's lovely," Mom says. Everything's lovely, apparently.

I'm still standing there, wondering if it's too soon to go change into bathing suits and jump in the pool. I wish Lauren and Bean would just leave already so I could have Claudia to myself.

"What a lovely tote," Mom says about this long bag that Lauren has over her shoulder. It's just a canvas tote with the word *Tranquility* embroidered in pink letters. It's nothing that special, really.

"Thanks. It's from Etsy." Lauren smiles. "It's basically the only place I shop these days."

"Oh, I know," Mom says. "It's just so fabulous that artists can sell directly to—"

"So, Mom, Grandma, Lucy," Claudia interrupts, thankfully, because this conversation about Lauren's tote bag was getting really boring for everyone except Lauren and Mom. "I know this may come as a shock to you, but it was a really last-minute decision."

I look at Claudia and then at Bean and I start to get a bad feeling.

Did they elope?

"I invited Bean to come stay with us for the summer."

I gasp. I feel like someone sucked all the water out of our perfect pool with a straw and there will never be water in it again. Everything I had been looking forward to just evaporated.

"What?" I ask.

Claudia ignores me and looks at Mom and Grandma, who haven't said anything. After a second she continues. "Bean has a great mind for business and he's going to be a huge help with the opening of the spa. His parents travel a lot for work, so there was really no point in him going back to Pittsburgh."

Grandma seems skeptical, but Mom nods like it's a totally genius idea.

"And we're in love," Claudia says, grabbing Bean's hand. "We're really in love."

"What?" I ask again. She cannot be serious. She's in love with Bean? First of all, what kind of a name is Bean? He's probably called that because he looks like a string bean. A long, skinny, dried-out string bean.

"Oh, that is wonderful, Claudia," Mom says. "I remember when your father and I felt like that. Like we could conquer the world together."

When Mom brings up Dad in this fairy-tale, romantic

comedy kind of way, I wonder why their relationship isn't like that now. I get all these hopeful thoughts and start to think that maybe it will be like that again someday. But I hate to think like that, because it means I'll just get my hopes up and then be disappointed again. Dad lives in England and has this big, important professor job there. I don't know if he'll ever be able to come back permanently, or even if he'd really want to.

Grandma shoots Mom a look and shakes her head. I can almost read her thoughts. They're saying: *And I remember when you had no money and lived here and had your head in the clouds.*

"Jane, may I have a word with you, please?" Grandma asks, and takes Mom's hand and leads her to the side of the house. I need to walk away too, so I go and join Sunny, Evan, and Yamir on the porch.

"What's going on?" Sunny asks. "And can we go swim? It's really hot out here."

I plop down on the porch, not even caring if I get any splinters in my legs. "Bean is staying with us for the summer. They're in love. Can you believe it?"

"Really?" Sunny asks.

Evan and Yamir don't have anything to say. Clearly they don't understand why this is a big deal.

"Yup. Unless my mom and grandma say no or something. But I doubt they'll do that."

"Maybe he'll be cool to have around," Sunny says. "Maybe he can be your chauffeur. You can even make him wear a hat and open doors for you."

I roll my eyes at her. "We don't have an extra car, but good thought."

No one else says anything. We're just sitting here staring at Claudia, Lauren, and Bean in the driveway. Bean looks nervous.

"Bye, Lucy," Lauren yells. "Nice to meet you!"

I wave good-bye and Lauren gets back in the car and drives away. Bean's and Claudia's bags are just sitting in the driveway now. If Grandma and Mom do say no to Bean staying, I have no idea how he'll get home. Lauren's off to her fabulous beach house and we're stuck with Bean.

We have so much work to do. The ground-breaking ceremony for the spa is tomorrow, and we waited until Claudia got home before having it. It's two weeks later than it should have been because she claimed she was busy setting up this summer camp for poor kids in Chicago. She was probably just busy spending more alone time with Bean.

"Eww," Sunny says, and we all look over to the driveway again. Claudia's giving Bean a massage, and it's grossing all of us out. "We're going to swim, OK, Lucy?"

"Fine," I groan.

"Do you want me to stay with you?" Yamir asks, and he has his nervous face on, the one that makes the left side of his mouth twitch a little.

I smile. I'm so proud of him for saying the right thing that it doesn't really matter if he stays or not. "No, it's OK. You can go swim."

"Is the code for the gate still 1818?" Sunny asks. My grandma is so paranoid about people drowning that we still have a gate for the pool, and she really doesn't like people to be back there without an adult.

"Yeah," I say. "Be really careful."

Mom and Grandma come back around and walk over to the driveway to talk to Claudia and Bean. Thankfully, Claudia has stopped the massage. It's too hot out for massages anyway. I don't know why you would want someone's sweaty hands on you.

I wonder if I should go over and join them. But I'm so annoyed that I'd rather stay here, in the shade of the porch, on one of the wicker rocking chairs. I can hear everything they're saying anyway.

"We really wish you had told us in advance," Grandma says. "There's so much going on with the spa opening that it's going to be hectic having someone else around the house. I wish I'd had time to prepare."

"I know, Grams," Claudia says. "But Bean won't be a hassle. He's a good cook too!"

"Oh, I'll be a huge help, Mrs. Desberg," Bean says. "I can cook, do laundry, go grocery shopping, drive people around, you name it."

"You're hired!" Mom says, and laughs, even though no one else does.

Grandma shakes her head at Mom and looks back at Claudia. "You have to know there are some ground rules," Grandma says. "Separate rooms. Bean can sleep in the attic guest room. I'll turn on the air-conditioning up there and take my winter clothes out of the closet."

"The attic? He can just sleep in the guest room on the second floor," Claudia says.

"No. I said the attic," Grandma says.

Grandma's a smart lady. The stairs up to the attic creak so loud, the whole neighborhood can hear them. She'll know if Bean's not where he's supposed to be.

Grandma continues, "And we need Bean pitching in."

"He said he would," Claudia says, looking at him.

Grandma leans in to whisper something in Claudia's ear. And then they walk off to the side a little bit. I bet it's about me. I bet she's telling her that they have to include me, and spend time with me, like I'm some kind of charity case.

Well, I'll show them. I'll be busy too, with Yamir and Sunny and Evan. We have plans to go to the beach and we'll be busy with the Earth Club stuff. Mrs. Deleccio wants us to come in a little over the summer to work on the Going Green school board proposal.

I try to eavesdrop, but I can't really hear much.

"Next time, we'll need a little more notice," Grandma says to Claudia, no longer whispering. "This isn't a hotel, and bringing a boyfriend home is a serious thing."

The thing is, Claudia's not the only one with a boyfriend. I sorta have one too. I mean, yeah, Yamir and I haven't come out and said it, really. We don't go around telling the whole world how in love we are or anything.

But I'm pretty sure he's my boyfriend. He looks out for me, pays attention to me. We see each other almost every day. It's in a group, but it's still seeing a lot of each other. So that's gotta mean something. I always get excited to see him, and it seems like he gets excited to see me too. That's really the most important sign of a good relationship, I think.

Their conversation ends and Claudia and Bean walk over to me. "Wanna go swim, Luce?" Claudia asks. "I've been practicing my dives. You're not even gonna believe my flip."

"Liar. You swim in Chicago?"

"Oh, does she swim!" Bean exclaims. "She's practically a fish."

I don't want to be happy; I want to stay mad at Bean for being here over the summer. But at this moment, all I can think about is the pool in the backyard and Claudia being home and dumping buckets of ice water on her stomach while she's sleeping on the lounge chair next to me.

It's summer. Claudia's home. The ground breaking for the spa is happening tomorrow. Even with Bean here, I have to be a little bit happy.

When Claudia's around, it's not just that everything feels better. Everything *is* better.

Lucy's tip for becoming a better person:
If you see someone before eleven A.M.,
say good morning.

I wake up ridiculously early the next day. This always happens to me when I'm really excited about something or really nervous about something. And in this case, it's both.

It's almost seven and no one else is up yet. I can't believe it. We have to be at the pharmacy by nine. Mayor Danes said to be prompt, and we can't just run in when all the news crews are there—it would look so unprofessional. Besides, they're going to want interviews and stuff. I can't look sweaty and frazzled.

I walk around upstairs and try to make as much noise as possible—loudly closing the medicine cabinet door, slamming down the toilet seat, flushing a few extra times. Nothing's working.

And then I hear creaking on the stairs from the attic to the second floor. And then I remember: Bean. Figures that Bean is the first one up. Now I'm going to have to see him all awkward in the morning in his pajamas with messy hair before he's brushed his teeth. It's grossing me out.

"Good morning, Lucy!" he says, so cheery. And then he does this weird salute thing that I don't really understand.

"Good morning," I mumble, not looking at him.

"Ready for your big day?"

I like the fact that he's calling it *my* big day, which it kind of is even though it's everyone's big day too, but I can't focus on that because all I'm thinking about is that he hasn't brushed his teeth yet. I am a brush-your-teeth-as-soon-as-you-get-up kind of person.

Soon everyone's getting up, and since I was awake and ready before everyone else, I take it upon myself to make breakfast. I scramble some eggs and fry some French toast and I even put a carton of orange juice in Mom's fancy pitcher. I want this to feel like a special day since it really, really is.

"Thanks for breakfast, Luce," Claudia says after a sip of juice. "So what exactly happens today? I was thinking I'd throw my beach stuff in the car, and Bean and I will probably go there for the afternoon."

"You're going to the beach?" I ask, with my mouth half-full of French toast.

Claudia makes a disgusted face. "Eww. Don't talk with your mouth full." She shakes her head at me like I've completely lost all sense. "Yeah, we're going to the beach. The ground breaking won't take all day."

I finish chewing and then speak. "Claudia, don't you realize how much work we have to do? This is just the official ground breaking, so construction has already started, but we still need to order everything, hire staff, all of that stuff." I look over at Bean to see if he'll agree with me. He's sipping coffee and reading the newspaper, and I bet he's not even listening.

"Relax, Lucy." Claudia smiles her you're-insane smile and pulls her chair back from the table.

A little while later, Mom, Claudia, and Bean are still doing who knows what in the house, so Grandma and I are waiting in the car for them.

"Lucy, doll," Grandma says, looking back at me from the front seat. "You know I am so unbelievably grateful for all that you did to help save the pharmacy, right?"

I nod. She's told me like a billion times. She's said over and over again how smart it was for me to apply for that Going Green grant and how entrepreneurial it was of me to start doing the makeovers and to create the Relaxation Room. I don't know why she's saying it again now.

"But here's the thing, love," she goes on, and I know that

17

whenever she starts a sentence like that, whatever follows will definitely not be good. "I don't expect you to totally take care of opening the spa on your own. What do we know about opening a spa? If we're going to do it right, we need a professional to help us, don't we?"

I'm not really sure what she's getting at. Is she telling me I'm fired? If you're not an official employee, can you really be fired anyway?

"You're still going to be a huge help, though," Grandma continues. "You'll be—"

"Hola, amigos!" Bean yells as he's getting in the car. "Doris, if you ever want me to drive, just say so. I have a clean driving record. I could be the Desberg chauffeur!"

I roll my eyes. "You mentioned that yesterday."

Grandma cracks up. "Thanks, Bean."

"OK, you can be the family driver, but only if you wear a uniform and a hat and call me m'lady," I add.

Grandma shoots me a look. "Lucy," she warns.

I wish Claudia would hurry up instead of leaving me in the backseat with her dumb boyfriend. He totally interrupted Grandma's train of thought when she was telling me what I'd actually be doing at the spa, since apparently I'm not "professional" enough to be in charge.

Finally Mom and Claudia come out. Bean slides over so

that he and Claudia can sit next to each other, which works to my advantage because Bean gets stuck in the awful middle seat. Plus, he's really tall, so the top of his head hits the roof.

I'm about to laugh when I notice that Claudia and Bean are holding hands, which makes the whole situation no longer funny, just ridiculous. They don't really need to hold hands right now, when we're all in the car together.

"I just got a text from Gary," Grandma says. Gary's our investor; he's known Mom and Grandma forever. "They'll be able to make it today after all."

It's still really funny to me that my grandma knows how to text. I wonder if all grandmas do, or if she's just incredibly hip.

"What? Really?" Mom asks. "Ugh, I needed to prepare for that. Gary's not a person you just spring on others."

"Yeah, not like Bean," I say sarcastically under my breath and then regret it.

"Lucy!" Claudia hisses.

Mom and Grandma are arguing in the front seat about Gary and I don't need to hear this same conversation for the millionth time. "Why is your name Bean, anyway?" I ask him.

"Well, my real name is Noah Beanerman, but everyone has always called me Bean."

"Even your parents?"

He laughs. "No, I mean, like my friends and stuff."

"Got it." Am I the only one who notices that he really does look like a string bean, though? He's so tall and thin. I think about bringing it up, but I'm not sure if Claudia would find it funny.

We get to the pharmacy and there are already a million people there, just like I thought there would be. OK, not exactly a million, but at least fifty or sixty. They're taking up the whole sidewalk, all the way down to the car wash.

My stomach starts getting that rumbly feeling and soon everyone's out of the car and off in a million directions and I don't even know where to go. It's my family's store, and for the first time I feel like I'm lost in it, like I don't know my way around.

I know Sunny and Yamir and their parents are coming, so I decide to make finding them my project. I hope that when I find them, Yamir is nice and supportive to me. Sometimes he's nice, but sometimes he's weird and aloof and only half-paying attention to me. That makes me wonder if we're boyfriend and girlfriend or not. It's not clear-cut like it is with Evan and Sunny or Claudia and Bean.

With Evan and Sunny, he basically just said he wanted to be her boyfriend one day when they were waiting on line to buy slushies at the movies. And she said OK, and it's been that way for two months now.

But with Yamir . . . nothing. We hang out and we have fun together, and sometimes I think we are boyfriend and girlfriend, but we might not be anything more than friends. It used to be that just being friends was good, and I liked the way things were, but is there something wrong that he doesn't want to be my boyfriend? Am I missing something?

Everyone's standing on the sidewalk in front of the pharmacy. As I'm about to walk in, someone hands me a hard hat, like I'm a real construction worker. This is what happens at ground-breaking ceremonies, so I put it on happily.

"Oh, Lucy, I'm so glad you're here!" I hear someone say, and turn around. It's a tall woman in a white sundress. "I'm Amelia, Mayor Danes's chief of staff. It's a pleasure to meet you." She shakes my hand while staring down at her iPad. "Your whole family is here now?"

I nod, still in awe of the fact that this woman does all of her work on an iPad. Does that make the clipboard obsolete? I always thought clipboards were so cool. But I have no idea why I am thinking about something as insignificant as clipboards at such an important time.

Amelia takes her cell phone (an iPhone, obviously) out of her dress pocket. "Phil," she says into the phone in half a second. I don't even know how it had time to ring on the other end. "The Desbergs are all here. Let's get started."

I'm still thinking about the fact that this super-important chief of staff woman knew who I was and recognized me, when I see Gary coming into the pharmacy.

Oh joy. Where's my mother? I need to warn her. I could say it in code, like "The eagle has landed" or something. She should know what that means.

"Lucy!" a little pip-squeaky, whiny voice yells, and then I see a short, chubby girl running up to me. One of her socks is higher than the other and she has a huge wet spot in the middle of her T-shirt. "Remember me? Bevin! We spent that whole afternoon having raft races in your pool that time we were eight. Remember?"

"Yeah. Hi, Bevin." I smile. "How are you?"

"I'm *grrrreat!*" she yells so loud that people turn around to look at us.

"OK, Lucy, we need you." Amelia grabs my arm and pulls me away. I wave good-bye to Bevin, but I'm relieved not to have to talk to her anymore.

Amelia leads me outside and that's where we find Mom, Grandma, Claudia, and Bean.

"Hello, Desbergs!" Mayor Dane, says, going down the line shaking each of our hands. "The day is here! Can you believe it?"

"Well, we began construction a month ago," Grandma says.

"But yes, we appreciate the town's commitment to our store and this wonderful celebration you guys are having for us."

"Of course, Doris." He smiles in his politiciany way.

It's funny because Grandma has known Mayor Danes since he was a little kid. He grew up in Old Mill and went to a school that was around the corner from the pharmacy. It was turned into a supermarket about ten years ago.

I wonder if it's hard for Grandma to take Mayor Danes seriously since she remembers when he would get milk mustaches at the pharmacy counter and count out his spare change to see if he had enough money to buy a pack of bubble gum.

Soon we all have our hard hats on and we're standing in front of the entrance of the pharmacy with Mayor Danes. There are a few news crews here and writers from the *Old Mill Observer* and the *Connecticut Chronicle*.

There are people standing all around us and when I look into the crowd, I spot Sunny, Yamir, and their parents. Sunny's waving at me and Yamir is looking down at his phone or his handheld game or something.

"Thank you all for coming out today for the official ground breaking of the Pink and Green Spa at Old Mill Pharmacy," Mayor Danes says into his megaphone, and everyone starts clapping. It's so loud that I wonder if people sitting in the movie theater are able to hear it. But then I remember that it's only nine thirty in the morning. I don't think movies ever start that early! "As I'm sure you all know, Old Mill Pharmacy is a local business that embodies community. It is where we go for prescriptions, where we go for advice when every lotion on the market will not help our dry skin." He pauses and everyone laughs. Who ever thought dry skin could be so funny? "But it is also where we go when we need some advice on anything from meddling mothers-in-law to the best method for making chicken soup. It is where we go for a smile after a hard day or a friendly face after a long winter. It is Old Mill's home away from home, and we are all so lucky to have it."

I look around the crowd again and I recognize so many of the faces—Meredith Ganzi and her mom from the movie theater down the street; Eli from the video store that the spa is expanding into; Mr. Becker and his baby son, Wyatt. Even my makeup client Courtney Adner and her parents came out. And everyone seems so happy to be here. It's early in the morning on a hot summer day and they're standing on the sidewalk, and yet they really seem happy.

"And now this pharmacy will be even more than a pharmacy," Mayor Danes continues. "It will be a spa. A place for beauty and rest and relaxation. And a green spa! Not only are the Desbergs of Old Mill Pharmacy saving us from life's pharmaceutical and everyday woes, but they are now saving the environment, too!"

After that there's more applause and I look around to see if I can find Mrs. Deleccio. She said she was going to come. After all, it's her Earth Club that got me into caring about the environment and the research during that club that helped me to find the Going Green grant for local businesses of Old Mill.

"And who would believe that the person behind all of this expansion and vision was a thirteen-year-old girl with a big heart and even bigger dreams?" Mayor Danes looks at me, and Claudia whispers in my ear, "He is *soooo* cheesy."

She's right, but she doesn't have to say it. He's saying amazing things about me, and I don't care if they're cheesy—I like hearing them.

"Thank you, Lucy, for all you have done, and all you will no doubt continue to do!" Mayor Danes says, and I bet if we weren't all already standing, people would give me a standing ovation. It just feels like that kind of moment. "So, let's all go inside, make sure your hard hats are on, and we will continue with the official ground breaking!"

I hope people don't mind that the wall between the pharmacy and the video store was already torn down and other walls for the treatment rooms have already been put up. I hope this ground breaking doesn't feel anticlimactic. We learned that word in English this year, and I think there are a lot of anticlimactic things in life. Come to think of it, Claudia coming home ended up being a little anticlimactic. I was all excited about it, and then . . . well, it hasn't been quite what I hoped for. But I guess that's just the way it is sometimes.

We all shuffle in and stand near the wall. Mom, Grandma, Claudia, and I are up front, and I'm glad that Bean is toward the back a little bit, because it means he realizes he's not part of the family. Not yet anyway.

The wall is mostly torn down and the archway is in the process of being remodeled, but we left a little bit up just for this purpose.

Mayor Danes hands me a sledgehammer. "Would you like to do the honors, Lucy?"

I look at Mom, Grandma, and Claudia and they're all nodding at me.

In my head I can hear Erica Crane saying something about how this is such a liability and her uncle who's a lawyer could totally report us or something else about the law and codes that really doesn't make any sense.

I quickly scan the crowd for her, but I don't see her. I'm relieved, even though I didn't really expect her to come.

"OK," I say, and I take the sledgehammer and slam it as hard as I can into that plaster wall. As I'm doing it, I'm imagining everything I've been angry about—Yamir acting dumb, Erica Crane being mean in Earth Club, my dad postponing his yearly trip to the United States, Claudia bringing Bean home for the summer. I guess I'm not very strong, because even using all of my strength, my hits don't do very much damage—barely any plaster falls off, and the hole isn't even very big—but as I'm hitting, all the anger I've been feeling seems to dribble away a little bit. I take one more slam and then put down the sledgehammer. I take a bow and everyone claps.

"Doris and Jane," Mayor Danes says, turning to face them. "Would you like to give everyone a little tour of the new space?"

"Phil," Grandma says, nudging him in her direction so she can say something to him quietly. "Is this safe? I mean, there's some loose flooring, a bunch of open wiring, and who knows what else?"

"It's OK, Dor," he says. "We do this all the time."

She shrugs.

"Follow the Desberg ladies!" Mayor Danes yells out to the crowd, and soon everyone's following us through the half-torn-down wall and the archway into the old Fellini & Friends video store.

It's hard to believe that within weeks, Pink & Green will really be open. Customers—brides-to-be, prom goers, bat mitzvah girls—will be coming in for makeup and massages and facials.

As we're walking in, I feel someone put their arms on my shoulders and when I turn around, I see that it's Sunny. She reaches over to give me a hug. "I am so proud of you, Luce! You really did it. Oh, and when did your mom and grandma agree to the name? You never told me it was officially going to be called Pink and Green."

I'm distracted as I'm talking to her because I'm looking around at everyone who is coming in with us, especially keeping an eye on Yamir. But I try to focus. "Well, the official name is 'Pink and Green: The Spa at Old Mill Pharmacy,' but everyone liked just 'Pink and Green' by itself. My grandma was worried people wouldn't know what it was, so she added that little bit at the end."

"Makes sense," Sunny says, peering around a corner. We've separated from the rest of the tour, but it's not like we really need to be with the group. I know my way around here. "That's the makeup chair?" she asks, pointing to a huge chair covered in plastic in the corner.

"Yup!" I walk over to it, and Sunny follows. "Isn't it so amazing? We ordered it special from this beauty supplies catalog. It has all these different settings, so I can make it higher or lower depending on how tall the people are."

"Let's unwrap it!" Sunny says.

"No, we can't. It'll get all dusty from the construction," I say. "But I promise you will be one of the first people to sit in it."

"Cool," Sunny says, seeming bored all of a sudden. I look away from the chair and back at her and I notice she's not even paying attention or seeming excited about the chair anymore. She's looking down at her phone, reading a text message or something. Finally she looks up. "Oh, sorry. Evan was just texting me, asking if I wanted to go to the carnival at Old Mill Elementary later."

"I thought they had one a few months ago."

"They did, but they're having another, and it's a fund raiser. They need money for that new music wing." She shrugs. "Should be fun, though."

Is Sunny really going to something and not inviting me? I don't know what to say. I just stay quiet. It'll come. She'll say *Do you want to come with us?* any second now.

But she doesn't. It feels like an hour goes by without either of us saying anything.

"Lucy, we need you," Grandma calls. "This lovely woman wants to ask you some questions."

"OK, so I gotta go, Sunny," I say, and give her one last chance to invite me.

"See you later! Go be your important spa-owning self." She smiles and blows me a kiss. But no invite.

𝒯he next few days seem to go in slow motion. I expected everything to happen superfast as soon as Claudia was home and we had the ground breaking, but instead it feels like I'm just sitting around all the time.

Every day I go to the pharmacy and help out with my usual stuff—the magazines, the hair products, keeping the Relaxation Room nice and neat—but I want to be doing stuff for the spa! I hang around the construction area and watch the workers handle the installations and the lighting and I page through spa catalogs, folding down corners.

Right now Mom and Grandma are in the back office looking at the calendar trying to figure the best day for the grand opening of the spa. I don't understand why they don't know the perfect day right away. It's so obvious.

I'm glad my eavesdropping skills have improved so

much and that I can hear them talking. I put the stack of magazines on the Relaxation Room table in a neat pile and run over to them.

"Hey, Lucy," Grandma says.

"Hi." I plop myself down on the office couch. "Whatcha talking about?" See, I can't make it too obvious that I'm a master eavesdropper, because if I do, they won't talk so loudly anymore and I'll never be able to hear what's going on.

"Just trying to figure out scheduling," my mom says, sounding worn out. "Ma, don't forget I have that wedding in August."

"What wedding?" I ask.

"Oh, a friend of Dad's and mine from Yale—her name is Esme. She and her fiancé live on a commune in New Hampshire. They're finally getting married," Mom says. "She's really crazy, but we—"

"OK." Grandma puts a hand on my mom's shoulder. "We don't need every single detail, Jane. Just remind me of the weekend."

"It's the weekend before Labor Day weekend. So we can do the grand opening before or after."

"Are you guys serious?" I ask. They look at me, confused. "It's ridiculously obvious that the grand opening of

Pink and Green needs to be Labor Day weekend. Hello, Boat Fest!"

Grandma raises her finger in the air like she's so excited about what I said, and then she pats me on the back. "Genius! My granddaughter, she's a genius."

I smile. "Well, how did you guys not think of that? I mean, all the fancy summer-home people are in town, lots of weddings go on over Labor Day weekend, and practically every single person in Connecticut is out and about that weekend!"

"OK, so it's settled!" Grandma declares. "Follow me."

We follow her over to the spa area. "Hey, Johnny," Grandma yells out over the noise of the drill and the sander and the other tools they're using. "Can we have everything ready to go by Labor Day?"

He turns off the drill. "Our part should be done, yeah. But y'all need equipment, lighting consults, all that other jazz."

I look at Grandma. I wonder if she realizes this is what I've been saying all along, but she doesn't look at me. She nods and Johnny turns the drill back on. We all cover our ears at the same time and leave the spa area.

"OK, time to return Gary's call," Grandma says. "He came into town for the ground breaking, but we didn't get a chance to chat. We need to make plans."

I look at my watch. Claudia was supposed to be here ten minutes ago to drive me to Earth Club. She's late. Since Bean's been here, she's always late.

"Ma, Gary's just the investor," Mom says to Grandma. "I don't think you need to consult him about every little thing." Mom's still stuck on the fact that she was set up with Gary years and years ago. I'm sure Gary's moved on and doesn't even think about it anymore, but for some reason my mom gets all weird whenever Gary's name comes up. Too bad for her, though, because Gary's a huge investor in Pink & Green, and I have a feeling he's going to be around a lot this summer.

Grandma ignores her and gets Gary on the phone. "Gary, hi, it's Doris." She pauses and waits for him to talk. "Oh, that's great," she goes on. "OK, well, fabulous, that's exactly what I was thinking. I'm glad you beat me to it." She nods. "And you're on top of compensation?" She's writing something down in her little red notebook. "Got it. See you tomorrow."

Grandma hangs up and Mom and I just sit there staring at her, waiting for her to tell us what that was all about.

"So, Gary's hired a spa consultant to help us get up and running," Grandma says, still writing stuff down in her notebook. "She's coming tomorrow, so we'll really start to get the ball rolling."

"But Grandma," I say, kind of in shock. "I know what we need to order. We don't need a consultant."

"Lucy," Grandma says in her letting-me-down-easy tone that I really, really hate. "We talked about this."

I should tell her that we started to talk about it but never really finished because Bean interrupted us.

Mom stands up and folds her arms across her chest. "Ma, who knows who this consultant is? She needs to know we're doing this all green. We can't just have any old person coming in here and telling us how to run the place."

"Relax, please. Both of you." Grandma sighs. "It's all going to be fine. Now, please excuse me so I can get back to the prescription counter. We are still a pharmacy, you know!"

Grandma leaves the office and my mom and I just stare at each other.

"Don't worry, Luce," my mom says. "You'll still play a huge part in the opening of the spa."

"Uh-huh," I grumble, then hear the car horn. "I gotta go to Earth Club. See you later."

I leave the pharmacy without saying good-bye to Grandma. She's busy filling prescriptions for the new local news anchor anyway.

Well, there's nothing I can do about the fact that both Grandma and Gary feel that the spa needs some kind of consultant. But I'll show them how much I can do. Let the consultant come. We can work together. She'll be so impressed with me. Grandma and Mom will be even prouder of me than they were when we got the grant. I'm not threatened by this spa consultant. Not at all.

"Hey," I say to Claudia and Bean when I get in the car.

"Hey, darlin'," Bean says. "We got you a surprise."

Claudia hands me one of those giant gobstoppers wrapped in waxed paper. "You used to love these," she says. "We saw them in a big bin at the mall, so we had to get one for you."

"That's sweet," I say, and crack up. "No pun intended."

I sit in the backseat and eat my gobstopper. I still can't believe that we actually agreed to work on school projects during the summer, but I guess it's OK because it's something we feel is important.

Today Earth Club is doing a beach cleanup. It's not exactly lounging at the beach, but it is better than sitting inside somewhere.

"Hey, you," I hear someone say as I'm walking through the entrance to the beach. Usually this is the place where you pay, but since it's a weekday before the height of the season, none of the guards are here.

It's Yamir. I could tell his voice anywhere, even with the sound of the ocean all around us.

"Hi," I say. "Waiting for Anthony?"

"No, I was waiting for you. Dummy." He hits his elbow against my arm.

"Oh." I smile. "That was nice."

"But now I have to wait for Anthony," he says.

I can't tell if he's serious or not, so I just wait to see what he does next. He sits back down on the bench. I'm actually a few minutes early to meet everyone by the lifeguard chair, so I sit with him.

"So what's new?" Yamir asks me.

"Ugh, everyone's annoying," I start. "Claudia's boyfriend is living with us for the summer and now Gary's hired this spa consultant, and I don't really have anything to do for the spa now, and no one cares about my ideas."

"Oh, boo-hoo, poor Lucy." He rolls his eyes. "You complain a lot. Did you know that?"

I stand up. "I'm going to find everyone now," I say, and start walking away from him. "You know we're here to clean, not just sit around, right?"

He doesn't respond.

I know I like to complain, but I never realized other people noticed how often I do it. It's not fun to have your bad habits pointed out. And I used to be such an optimistic person. It's just that now it seems like no one even cares if I'm around. Claudia is busy with Bean, and Sunny and Evan are lovebirds who are just happy hanging out with each other. And Mom and Grandma don't even really need my help around the pharmacy anymore. The grant led to all this awesome publicity, which led to business picking up, so they were able to hire our beloved pharmacy workers Tory and Charise back.

I'm practically useless to everyone.

"Lucy, what are you doing?" Mrs. Deleccio runs up to me. I decided to walk along the boardwalk for a few minutes before meeting up with everyone. I guess Mrs. Deleccio saw me and got worried. "We need you. There's more beach littering than you'd think; we have a lot to do."

I nod. "OK, I'm coming."

"I was really impressed with that organic food supplier you found," she says as we're walking over to the rest of the group. "And it seems like you're able to negotiate with them to get us a good rate, right?"

"Uh-huh."

"Lucy, you know you're an instrumental member of this club, right?" Mrs. Deleccio says when we're a few feet from everyone else. "I hope you'll still be able to give it your all even though you'll be really busy with the spa opening." She smiles at me. It's like she read my mind or sensed how I was feeling, but she said exactly what I needed to hear. Sometimes teachers just know these things; it's like they have psychic powers or something.

But the thing is, I want to be instrumental in other areas of my life too. Earth Club is barely even meeting over the summer; it can't be the only thing I work on. And maybe the pharmacy doesn't need me anymore, and the spa work is above my head. But I can do something else. I know I can. I just have to figure out another project, somewhere else I'm needed.

I walk over to the group, and Sunny and Evan are off to the side laughing about something.

"Hey, guys," I say.

"Oh hey, Luce," Sunny says. "Where's Yamir? He said he was waiting for you."

"He was." I pick up a shell and tell myself not to take any shells home, as much as I want to. I have so many shells at home already. "But then he said he had to wait for Anthony."

"Dummy." Evan crinkles his brow. "Anthony's not coming today. I just told him that. I bet he's just too lazy to actually do the beach cleanup."

I shrug.

"OK, Earth Club!" Mrs. Deleccio yells. It's very windy, so she needs to be loud to get our attention. "We're going to cover the strip of beach from this red flag to the one all the way down there." She points to the red flag on the far end, near the snack bar. "Meet back here in about a half hour. I have garbage bags for each of you." Mrs. Deleccio hands us each a garbage bag and I start walking toward the water to pick up trash that may have washed up during high tide. I look behind me to see if Evan and Sunny are close by, but they're traipsing behind.

"Are you guys coming?" I ask Evan and Sunny. They just keep cracking up. I have no idea what's so funny. I stop for a second and wait for them to catch up.

"Hello, I am Mr. Shell," Evan says, holding a shell and talking to Sunny. He bursts out laughing. Sunny does too, like he just said the funniest thing she's ever heard.

Sunny's holding up a shell too. "Hello, I am Mrs. Shell."

I don't know why they find the silliest things funny. They're acting like two little kids, and I really don't get it. And they obviously don't even care that I'm here.

I walk away. I can collect litter on my own. Maybe a quiet walk along the beach by myself will be good to clear my head.

Yamir comes down to the beach and catches up with me, with only about twenty minutes left before it's time to go.

"Sorry," he says. "I was confused. Anthony's actually not coming." He walks along with me, but doesn't get a garbage bag of his own. Instead, he puts whatever trash he finds in my bag.

"Uh-huh." I'm not really paying attention to him.

"Anyway, do you want to go see that new Spielberg movie next week?"

"What's it about?" I try not to act too excited about the fact that Yamir's asking me to hang out. It's been forever since we hung out alone, and I didn't even think he noticed.

"Kids solving this mystery about this campground or something," he says. "It looks freaky but not too scary."

I finally look at him. He looks so cute with his dark shaggy hair and his long eyelashes. "Sure, I'll go."

"Cool. Movie times aren't out yet, but I'll let you know."

"Yamir, I notice you don't have a garbage bag," Mrs. Deleccio says, coming out of nowhere. "If you're going to be here, I'd like you to participate."

"On it, Mrs. Deleccio." He stands up and marches over to the box of garbage bags, and takes one.

Mrs. Deleccio sighs.

"Mr. Shell, do you like living at the beach?" Sunny asks in this fake British accent.

I try to tune them out and focus on other things.

Mrs. Deleccio said I'm an instrumental part of this club, and I try to believe her. I really care about this, and even if I'm not needed at the pharmacy, I am needed here.

And Yamir asked me to go to the movies. Things aren't so bad. Maybe a little bit of an optimistic attitude would go a long way.

Lucy's tip for becoming a better person:
As hard as it is, try to put yourself in someone else's
shoes, and see how they might be feeling.

I don't ever knock on wood because I'm Jewish and my grandma told me once that Jews don't knock on wood. But sometimes I feel like I need something to ward off bad luck. Like right now. I want to knock on wood because things seem like they're working out, getting better even, and I feel like if I don't knock on wood, I'm taking it for granted and they could fall apart again.

Before we got the grant, I made this pact with God that if we got the grant and things worked out and we were able to open the eco-spa, then I wouldn't complain again. Even when I was making the pact, I knew it was kind of ridiculous and that I wouldn't be able to keep it because I sort of like to complain. Not to be annoying but to let off steam. But I made the pact anyway, hoping that just the fact that I made it would help keep me from complaining.

Anyway, every time I get down about stuff, I try to remember the pact and I try to think about knocking on wood (but not actually knock on it) because, basically, I just don't want to take any good things for granted.

I'm having this deep conversation with myself as I'm getting dressed and ready to leave for the pharmacy to meet Gary and the new spa consultant.

I remind myself about how nice it was for Claudia and Bean to think of me and get me the gobstopper and drive me around everywhere, and I'm also thinking about something else.

Yamir asked me to the movies. It's a big deal.

He didn't ask Sunny and Evan to come too. At least I don't think he did, because Sunny didn't mention it and she usually mentions these things immediately.

He asked me. One on one. And it's actually a movie I'm pretty interested in seeing, not something weird like aliens that creep into your brain or elevators that come alive and swallow you whole. That was the last movie he was obsessed with.

"Lucy, five minutes and we're going," Grandma yells to me from downstairs.

"OK!" I call back.

I usually don't take this long to get ready, but this fancy spa consultant person is coming from New York City and I bet she's going to look all chic, and I can't just stand there in my cutoff shorts and a pocket tee. I need her to take me seriously.

I walk downstairs and decide to take a granola bar on my way out for breakfast. It's not the kind of breakfast Mom usually approves of, but I took so long to get dressed and I don't want to be the one responsible for making us late.

"Lucy!" Claudia says as soon as she sees me, and then Bean does that obnoxious whistle thing that guys do to girls sometimes, even though he's totally doing it in a joking way. "You're so decked out."

"I'm not! It's just a sundress." I shake my head and turn away from them, but I can still hear them whispering.

"You look like you're going to a wedding," Claudia says. "Go change."

"Oh, Claudia, leave her alone," Mom mumbles, still half-asleep. Her hair is all frizzed and tied back into a ponytail. She's wearing one of those T-shirts that are meant to look faded, but hers looks a little too faded. "Be nice to your sister."

"I am being nice!" Claudia grabs one of my spaghetti straps and pulls me back closer to her. "I'm being nice because I'm being honest, and you look too overdressed to be going to spend a day on a construction site. You're wearing heels!"

I inch away from her and go out to the car. So what if I look overdressed? I want to wear this. And Claudia doesn't know I have flip-flops in my backpack and my hoodie to wear over my dress. The pharmacy gets freezing in the summer anyway. This outfit is just to make a good first impression.

When we get to the pharmacy, there's a town car pulled up in front and people are getting out of it. If Gary and the spa consultant really took a car service all the way from New York City, she's even fancier than I thought.

We drive into Grandma's regular spot in the parking lot and hop out of the car. Bean has his headphones on and I wonder if I should tell him to take them off. Claudia should probably be the person to do that, but she's not. And why is Bean even here? Claudia says he comes to the store so he can learn about business and stuff for his major, but I don't see him taking any notes. He spends most of the day staring at the mini fountain in the Relaxation Room.

"Hello, Gary!" Grandma says, and reaches out to hug him.

"Doris, you look more and more beautiful each time I see you," Gary says, and I hear Claudia mumble the word *barf* under her breath. Bean starts laughing, of course, because he laughs at everything my sister says, and then everyone looks over at us.

And that's when I notice it's not just Gary and the spa consultant getting out of the car. There's someone else here. Bevin. Gary's obnoxious daughter, who was born three days after me. She should be back home by now. She came for the ground breaking, but I figured that would be it.

"Lucy!" Bevin screams so loud that my mom covers her ears. "I am so so so so so so so excited to see you. We didn't really get to talk the other day."

She runs over and hugs me and I just stand there being hugged, not hugging her back. But if I act like she's acting, the spa consultant won't take me seriously.

"We have so much to catch up on," Bevin says. "We haven't really talked since we were in sixth grade."

"That was only, like, a year ago," I say to Bevin.

She doesn't seem like she hears me. "And I told everyone in my school about how you saved the pharmacy, and they were all, like, really impressed. They think you're *sooooo* cool."

"Why don't we all go into the Relaxation Room so we can sit down and discuss the plans?" Grandma says, like it's an instruction and not a suggestion. "It's right over there. Lucy can show you the way."

I nod. Phew. For a second I thought Grandma was going to make me take Bevin to another part of the store and work on cleaning or something just to entertain her. But no! I'm part of the discussion because I'm part of this business. If anyone should be entertaining Bevin, it should be Bean, the interloper.

We all sit down on the Relaxation Room couches and Mom brings over a tray with pretty little mugs and her floral teapot, which is probably her most prized possession.

"Green tea," my mom says. "Who would like some?" She's talking in her quiet voice. She woke up two hours ago, but I know she's not really awake yet.

Everyone says they'd like some, and Bean runs back to the office to get some more mugs. It's good to see him making himself useful.

"Our goal is to open the spa Labor Day weekend," Grandma says. "That's a really big weekend around here." She's talking directly to Gary and the spa consultant. And that's when I realize I don't even know this person's name.

"I'm sorry to interrupt," I say to her. "But I didn't introduce myself. I'm Lucy, Doris's granddaughter."

"Lovely to meet you, Lucy." She smiles. Her teeth are insanely white and perfectly straight. "I'm Anais."

She's probably one of the prettiest people I've ever seen in my life. She's got clear, dark skin, and she's wearing a long white skirt and a beaded black tank top. She looks like the kind of person who never sweats. I want her to like me. I want to work with her. I want her to think I know what I'm talking about, or *know* that I know what I'm talking about.

Anais crosses and uncrosses her legs and looks down at

her notebook. "Well, there's a lot of work to do. I'm glad the construction has begun. From what I can tell, the rooms are already done. We need to work on the waiting area, get all of the furniture, supplies, etc. And then of course we need to work on marketing, signage, all of that."

Mom nods. "I'm in charge of all the publicity. I've already reached out to the local papers. I've gotten in touch with my contacts. I'd love to work with you on the best design for the sign, stationery, all of our branding stuff." Mom pauses and sips her tea. She immediately winces, which must mean she has burned her tongue.

"Excellent."

Anais is writing in her notebook when Grandma looks at Gary and says, "So, Gar, what's your plan, your role in all of this?"

He puts his mug down on the table and when a little tea spills, he wipes it up with the sleeve of his flannel shirt. Yes, he's wearing flannel in late June. I can see why Mom's really not into him.

"Well, Dor, to be honest, it's a little much to travel back and forth from the city so often. I was looking into renting a place here for the summer, but they're pretty pricey. I guess things have changed since I was a kid." He picks at his chin hair and it's grossing me out so much that I have to look away.

"And I really want to be involved with everything. I know you're in good hands with Anais; she's done this many times. She helped open the Great Jones Spa in Manhattan, one of the best in the world. But I'd still love to be here if I can."

Mom's flipping through one of Anais's spa supplier catalogs, and Claudia and Bean are trying to discreetly play the can-knock-down game on Bean's iPad.

"It's settled, then," Grandma says to Gary, and I notice I'm the only one paying attention. Bevin has fallen asleep in the Turbo Massage Chair 7000. I don't think she realizes it's still on and massaging her back. "You'll move into the upstairs apartment. It's cleaned out and everything; we scanned all the paperwork so it's digital now and so it's no longer needed for storage."

"What?" I ask, but no one hears me.

"I've got Bevie with me for the summer. Her mom's on some photography assignment in Senegal." He rolls his eyes and I look over at Bevin to make sure she's still asleep. I know how it is when one parent is annoyed at the other parent. Just two weeks ago we found out that my dad's trip to the United States was postponed because of extra teaching commitments. He comes every year at the end of June when school's out, and he usually spends two weeks or more. He stays at this amazing bed-and-breakfast on the water, and he gets a suite so Claudia and I can have our own room. It's usually the best time ever. My dad is honestly a kid disguised as a grown-up—he always gets waffles with ice cream for breakfast and encourages us to do the same. He stays up late, and if it's raining, he takes us to see three or four movies in a day!

He apologized a million times and I said it was OK, and that I understood, but deep down I'm so disappointed, and kind of mad too.

The thing is, I was really little when he first moved away to England, and so I didn't really get it. But now I do get it, and I miss him, and I wish he were here more. So his visits are extra-important.

And if he's going to just postpone his trip like it's no big deal, how can I ever really trust him? I think all of these things but I can never say them out loud—not even to Claudia or Sunny.

"There are two bedrooms up there!" Grandma says, like Gary's an idiot and he should have known that. "Bring Bevin, she can hang out with Lucy and Claudia. It'll be great. We'll put her to work, though, I'm warning you now."

"What?" I ask again, louder this time, but still, no one's paying attention.

What is wrong with these people?

Grandma ignores me, and Anais is still writing down notes.

I can't imagine what she's writing, but she's gotten up three times to go look at the spa area and no one's even noticed.

"Oh, Dor, wouldn't that be a huge nuisance?" Gary asks.

Yes, yes it would be! I'm screaming in my head, but I'd never be so rude to scream that out loud. Why did Grandma just offer that? Has she totally lost her mind? Did Mom put some crazy ginseng or something in the green tea?

Grandma waves her hand in that *pshaw* way people do when the other person is saying something outlandish. "Not a bit. But you'll kick in a little rent, maybe that'll ease your mind?" Grandma smiles. "I know we got the grant, thanks to Lucy, and this spa is very exciting, but money's still tight, you know."

"Ma! Enough with that!" Mom finally tears herself away from the spa supplier catalog. "How many times in my life am I going to hear you say that?"

"That's fair," Gary says.

"So it's settled then," Grandma says, completely ignoring Mom's comment. "Go back to Manhattan, get your stuff, move in whenever. OK, back to business." She turns to look at Anais.

Mom and I are staring at each other, wondering if what happened is what we think happened.

What on earth am I going to do with Bevin all summer?

"I've made a list," Anais says, pouring herself another cup of tea. "I can see, and also Gary has told me, that this is truly a family business. You all want to be involved, and that is wonderful. I've divvied up responsibilities, and then you can tell me if the fits seem right."

I nudge Claudia with my elbow and they finally turn off the iPad and pay attention. Bean is such a bad influence on her. She could do so much better, but now isn't the time for me to tell her that.

Anais stands up and does some yoga-like stretching and then begins reading off the list. Bevin is still asleep. Clearly she's not going to be much help around here, but that's OK with me. I can do it fine on my own.

"Jane will be in charge of the publicity and the branding. She has connections to local news sources and she has an eye for design, I can tell from the wonderful relaxing atmosphere in here." She looks over at Mom and Mom starts to say, "Well, that was really Lucy's doing," but then Grandma shuts her up, and Anais goes on.

"Claudia and Lucy and Bevin, if she's here, will be in charge of the hiring process. I've spoken to Claudia about this and she seems up for the task. Gary and I will be making the final decisions, but you can do the initial groundwork." Anais looks at Claudia.

"Bean can help us with that too." Claudia smiles. "His dad is the vice president of HR for JetBlue."

"Got it." Anais pulls her hair into a low ponytail. "Doris, Gary, and I will oversee the operations, handle the supplies, setting everything up, and preparing for the grand opening. And you'll keep running the actual pharmacy." She looks down at her notebook one more time. "Any questions?"

"I'll also oversee the eco-spa aspect of it, focusing on the eco," Mom says. "That was Lucy's vision, that's why we got the grant in the first place, and we must make sure that everything is up to the correct environmental standards." Mom looks at me. "Right, Lucy?"

"Right."

"OK, I will make a note of that," Anais says. "So if we're in agreement, I'd like us to all walk over to the spa area together, and we can discuss how we envision the entrance area."

Gary goes over to the Turbo Massage Chair 7000 and taps Bevin on the arm. "Bevie," he whispers. "Come on. Get up."

Bevie? If he keeps calling her that, it's going to get very annoying.

As we're walking over to the spa area, Grandma whispers to Mom, "Anais is great, isn't she?" For the first time in a while, Grandma actually seems relaxed. Even though every single thing about this spa opening is annoying me, I'm happy to see Grandma relaxed. I need to appreciate that.

"She seems very amenable to us all working together," Mom admits. "And she's very calming."

"I agree," Grandma says, and she puts her arm around Mom.

Deep breaths, Lucy. Deep breaths. I say that to myself over and over again. I can't always be complaining, like Yamir said I was.

Anyway, things aren't so bad. Anais understands that we all have a role here. It's going to be OK.

And based on today, Bevin will probably be sleeping the whole summer anyway.

Anais is the kind of consultant who's always traveling. She'll help open a spa in Boston one month and then be sent to Arizona to open a spa there the next month. Her housing is paid for by her company, and I have to admit . . . it's my dream job. I know I talked forever about becoming Laura Mercier and having my own makeup line and everything, but guess what? I'm thirteen and I can change my mind. Or maybe I can have two dream jobs for now, and then decide when I actually have to work.

Right this minute, I want to be a spa consultant and travel all over the country—and the world. Anais said she was helping a spa in Paris a few months ago. Paris! Unbelievable.

The best part about Anais being here is that we don't have to pay her anything. I didn't realize this until I overheard Grandma, Mom, and Gary talking the other day. Gary was saying how her salary is included in his part of the investment. He wants to make sure the spa gets off to the best start possible. And I agree 100 percent. For once, Gary and I are on the same page.

Gary and Bevin are moving into the upstairs apartment today, and Anais is moving into her apartment. The Fourth of July is this weekend, and then we will have less than two months to get the spa open. That's not that long. It feels like after today things are going to go really, really fast.

Claudia put an ad online that the soon-to-be-opened Pink & Green: The Spa at Old Mill Pharmacy is looking for employees: facialists, makeup artists, waxers, and all kinds of aestheticians and beauticians.

She's really good at writing stuff like this, and Bean said he knew how to word it since he's helped his dad with human resources stuff before. I wanted Anais to look it over, but she said it was OK to start out and she'd help us if we needed it.

We're waiting for the first interviewee to arrive when my phone starts buzzing in my pocket.

"Whatcha doing?" Sunny asks me when I answer. "I'm so bored."

"Where's Evan?" I ask, and I know I've got an attitude, but the truth is, she pretty much spends all her time with him anyway.

"At his grandparents' in the Berkshires for a few days," she grumbles. "See why I'm bored?"

She doesn't even try to pretend that Evan hasn't pretty much replaced me. Sunny doesn't understand that's something she should try to do.

"Sorry. I'm busy, Sunny. We have an interview coming in."

"Fine." She stops talking like she's waiting for me to change my mind. "Call me later. OK?"

"Sure." I won't say this out loud or anything, but I'm not going to call Sunny a million times over these next few days while Evan is away. I want her to miss me.

Mom and Grandma are helping Gary and Bevin move in upstairs, and every other minute I hear something drop and Mom or Grandma curse and then yell at each other for a few seconds. I'm glad I'm not up there right now. But I kind of wish I was helping Anais move into her apartment. She's renting this place right on the water. You walk outside the main door to her apartment building and there's the ocean. And they also have a pool for the people who live there. It sounds like paradise, but it's right in Old Mill, Connecticut. But when I asked if she needed help, she told me she's all set. Her company even pays for movers and unpackers and people who set up her electronics and everything.

See what I mean? Dream job.

"Hello, I'm looking for . . . uh . . . ," a girl says as she's walking into the pharmacy and then she looks down at a crumpled slip of paper. "Claudia Deszszsberg." She doesn't know how to pronounce our name. Few people do. It's Desberg, with a soft *s*, but some people pronounce it with a *z* sound.

"Hello, I'm Claudia." My sister reaches over to shake her hand. Claudia's wearing a gray pencil skirt and a crisp white button-down. Does she realize she's not the one being interviewed? No one told me to dress up. I'm in khaki capri pants and a striped T-shirt. But even Bean looks dressed up, or as dressed up as Bean can really look. His camel cargo pants are a little wrinkly and so is his button-down, but at least he's wearing a tie. It has pink flamingos on it, but it's still a tie. It's obvious he tried.

"A pleasure to meet you, Claudia," the girl says, a little more relaxed. "I'm Diana. I have a ten-thirty appointment."

Claudia nods. "Of course. Right this way."

Claudia and Bean lead Diana through the pharmacy to the spa area, where there's a tiny little meeting room. It's barely set up, but Anais made sure there was a small couch, two rolling desk chairs, and ample lighting. I follow behind them.

"It's still very much in progress, as you can tell," Claudia says.

Diana sits down on the little love seat and Bean and

Claudia get to the rolling desk chairs before me. Then I'm left standing, not knowing what to do. I look over at Claudia, but she's already staring down at the list of questions we came up with last night.

"So tell us about your experience at the Coral Reef Spa in Florida," Claudia starts. "You were there a while?"

Diana opens her mouth to answer, but they can't expect me to just stand for the whole interview so I say, "Um, I'm just going to go find another chair." All three of them look up at me and then go back to what they're doing.

I go scavenging around the spa area for another chair, but I know I won't find one there. I'll just go take Mom's chair from the pharmacy office and return it when I'm done. Mom won't mind since she's busy helping Bevin and Gary move in.

I can't believe this. Claudia acts like I'm so important and such a vital part of the spa. But that's only when the grown-ups are there. When it's actually time to do something, she pretty much ignores me. She and Bean planned to dress up and look all professional for the interview, but they never told me! They wanted me to look young in my ratty clothes, and they planned for me to not have a seat. This is a conspiracy! A conspiracy for me to quit working at the spa and go find some kid activity to do. Well, it's not gonna happen.

I'll bring my own chair if I have to!

That reminds me of one of Claudia's friends who didn't get into Yale. It was her dream her whole life, and she's kind of an "outside-the-box thinker." She was so determined to get there somehow that she purchased a folding chair and a lap desk and wrote a letter to the dean. She included the receipts for the purchases with the letter and basically said something like: "I will attend Yale, and sit in the back of the room, on my own chair, not disturbing anyone. Thank you."

They ended up letting her in after she reapplied the next year, and she's doing really well so far. That's what Claudia told me anyway.

That's just one of those stories that proves someone can really do what she sets her mind to. So if people don't want to include me in the opening of this spa, then I will literally bring my own chair! I will make it happen!

I'm walking over to grab the chair when I get a text from Sunny.

SO BORED. PLEASE HELP.

It seems to me Sunny should have more of my "bring your own chair" philosophy and find something to do.

I'm about to barge into the office to grab Mom's desk chair when I notice the door is closed, and then I hear voices.

"Lucy's asked me seven times when you're coming," I hear my mom say, and when I don't hear anyone say anything back, I figure out what's going on. She's on the phone with my dad. "Please do not disappoint her. Claudia doesn't care; she's busy with her boyfriend. But Lucy was really looking forward to your visit."

That's not true—Claudia cares too. She's just not as open about it as I am. I wish I knew what they're talking about. It could be scheduling or—worst-case scenario—maybe Dad's moved on and has a new family. It seems out of the blue, but I guess it could happen.

"Oh, that's an idea!" Mom says, and I can tell even through the closed door that she's excited. She gets that high-pitched squeak in her voice only when she's excited about something. I love that squeak.

"She would freak, Sam," Mom continues. "You know she would." She pauses for a second and I wish so much that I could see her facial expression right now. "But then how much time would you really have with the girls?"

Silence again. If I wait any longer, I'll miss Diana's whole interview. I need to get that chair. I need to be in that interview so Bean and Claudia know that I care.

I knock on the door and then I hear Mom say, "OK, Sam, I gotta run. E-mail me your tentative plans and I'll go from

there. I think we still have a few weeks until the RSVP date."
She hangs up and then sings, "Come in!"

"I need a chair," I say right away so she doesn't think I've
been listening. "Claudia and Bean didn't even get me one for
the interview. And they didn't tell me they were dressing up."

Mom's sitting there, staring at me, and then it occurs to
me that complaining like a little kid won't help them take me
more seriously. It will just remind them that I'm a kid.

"Anyway, can I borrow your chair?"

"Take Grandma's," Mom says, but she's already turned
back to the computer, looking at that site that lists every air-
line's flight prices. "Oh, Luce, I probably won't see you later.
I have that Green Entrepreneurs lecture this afternoon. Give
me a kiss."

I kiss my mom on the cheek and peek over at the computer. There's a minimized tab on the bottom of her screen
that appears to be an e-mail, with the subject heading "RE:
summer plans."

My dad's up to something. It could be a big surprise, like
maybe he's coming to Connecticut to pick us up and then
take us on a cruise around Europe. Or maybe even a cruise
to Europe. But there isn't really time for all that, not with the
opening of the spa in less than two months.

Well, he's got to be planning something, that's for sure.

And as long as he's planning something, I know he's thinking about us. And if he's thinking about us, I know he cares.

By the time I get back with Grandma's desk chair, Claudia, Bean, and Diana are shaking hands again. "We'll be in touch," Claudia says.

"Thanks again. This is going to be an amazing spa," Diana says as she's walking out.

Claudia and Bean leave the spa and plop down in the Relaxation Room. "She seemed smart," Claudia says. "But I think she may be too expensive."

Bean nods. "Yeah, she has tons of experience. Of course she's expensive."

They look at each other for a few seconds.

"So when's our next interview?" I ask.

"Luce, we can handle this. And you really don't know anything about interviewing people," Claudia says in her fake-sweet voice, like she's trying so hard not to hurt my feelings. "I'm sure there are other things you can help with. Just ask Anais."

"She said I should help with interviewing."

"Fine." Claudia turns away from me. "Be stubborn. But please be quiet. Our next interview is in twenty minutes, and we want to take a power nap."

Please. They're so tired after one interview? They didn't

even wake up today until nine A.M. I was up at eight, making coffee for them and Mom and Grandma. I'm the only one who seems too excited to sleep, and yet I'm being left out of everything.

I leave Claudia and Bean to their nap, and if they don't wake up in time for the next interview, I'll just do it myself. That'll show them.

I walk back over to the pharmacy and I quickly tidy up the facial products aisle and the makeup aisle. We can't have it looking like a total mess if we're interviewing people for the spa. Those aisles will be the first place they look!

I hear the door chimes and I look up thinking it's the next interviewee, but it's actually Anais.

"Anais!" I jump up and walk over to her. "How's moving in?"

"Fine, Lucy." She smiles, but it seems forced, not relaxed like I'd seen her up until now. "Where's your mom?"

"Some Green Entrepreneurs conference," I say. "Can I help you with something?"

She smiles that forced smile again. "Where's your grandma?"

I shrug. "I can help you, I'm sure. I know everything about this place."

"Thanks, Lucy, but we actually have a small issue with

scheduling the inspection for the spa." She pauses. "I really need to speak to an adult. Have you seen Gary?"

"Nope. Sorry."

I leave her in the middle of the makeup aisle. I get why she needs to speak to an adult, because obviously I don't know anything about inspections, but it still stings. I decide to play a computer game while I wait for the next interview.

I'm beating the computer at Scrabble better than I've ever beaten it before when I get interrupted by a text. Why is Sunny bothering me again?

But when I look at my phone, I see that it's not from Sunny. It's from Yamir.

My stomach starts doing flips, like the kind Claudia can do off the diving board. I'm excited, then nervous, then excited again.

Gotta bail on the Spielberg movie. Clint's dad got free passes to a screening in NYC.

I should have expected this. Clint's dad does lighting for movie shoots and he always gets free passes. Why did I even get excited in the first place?

"Hey, Lucille," Bevin says, and she plops herself down on the office floor. She knows my name isn't Lucille, but for some reason she always feels the need to call me that. I really don't understand it.

I don't answer her.

"Whatcha doin', Lucille?"

"Playing Scrabble," I grumble.

My whole summer flashes before my eyes—it won't be like I planned, hanging out with Claudia, swimming, working at the pharmacy, and getting the spa ready. No. It'll be me hiding in the office while the grown-ups do cool stuff, and then Bevin coming to bug me. And Yamir won't even want to hang out with me. And Sunny will be busy with Evan.

"Can I play?" Bevin asks.

"It's a solo game and I play against the computer." I talk to Bevin while staring at the computer screen. I don't feel like being nice right now.

"What's wrong, Lucille?" Bevin takes a pen off Grandma's desk and starts drawing on her hand.

Aren't we a little old for pen tattoos?

"Nothing."

"Liar."

"I'm fine, Bevin, but thanks."

"Liar again."

Bevin might be the most annoying person on the entire planet. And of course she finds me to hang out with because she probably knows no one else can stand her. Either that or she figures they're all busy and I'm just a kid, so what do I have to do, just like everyone else thinks.

"Just tell me."

Finally I turn around. She's not going to stop until I say something. "Fine. If you must know, I'm annoyed that people still don't take me seriously around here, even though I'm the one who found the grant and got this whole spa thing going in the first place! And I'm annoyed that Claudia's busy with Bean and Sunny's busy with Evan and I'm totally left out of everything. And I'm annoyed that Yamir, who I think is my boyfriend but I don't really know for sure, asked me to go to the movies and then totally bailed so he could go with Clint!"

Bevin gets up and closes the office door. I guess she's worried everyone's going to hear me yelling, but I don't really care, and I'm done now anyway.

She sits back down on the floor. "OK." She takes a deep breath. "First of all, you have a boyfriend and I didn't even know that. So. Tell. Tell everything."

I squint at her. With everything that's going on, what's most important to her is Yamir. Strange.

"You're so lucky." She's braiding the threads on her cutoffs. "He must be really cool."

"Thanks," I say. "But maybe he doesn't even think he's

my boyfriend. I don't know. Sunny and Evan hang out all the time, but Yamir and I rarely do."

She shrugs. "So invite him to hang out! Invite him over to the pharmacy. Tell him to bring friends." She smiles. "Imagine if I met a boyfriend in Connecticut this summer and then I could go back and tell everyone at school. That would be amazing."

This conversation makes me realize that Bevin is even more pathetic than I am, which in a really, really mean way kind of makes me feel better.

Lucy's tip for becoming a better person:

Ask people questions. It shows you're interested.

$\mathcal{E}$very time $\mathcal{I}$ asked Mom and Grandma about the inspection scheduling problem that Anais was freaking out about, they told me that everything was fine.

I have this weird feeling that I shouldn't believe them, but I'm not going to worry about it now. It's the Fourth of July, one of my favorite holidays, and I can't waste it worrying!

I check my e-mail one last time before we head out for our big Fourth of July celebration. I get really excited when I see I have an e-mail from my dad.

Hey Lulu!
Just wanted to wish my girl a happy 4th o' July. I know it's your favorite, and it's sad to be somewhere that doesn't celebrate it.
Stay tuned for details about our reunion!

Oodles of Noodles,

Dad

Well, that didn't say much at all. But at least he's thinking about me today. It's pretty much more important to me than my own birthday, even! I wonder what he means by details and why he's being so vague. But I can't spend my day worrying about this—as frustrating as it is. It's the Fourth of July and we have a huge evening planned.

Anais's apartment is right on the beach where the Fourth of July fireworks are taking place, so she invited us all over for a champagne toast before. I try to put all of my frustration about being left out of things at the spa out of my mind.

"Are you always this chummy with the spa families you're working with?" I ask her, after a sip of my sparkling apple juice.

"Lucy," Claudia says in her I'm-horrified tone, but I really don't understand why that was such an inappropriate question.

Anais laughs. "No, no, that's a good question." She smiles at me and I look over and glare at Claudia. Since Bean's been living with us, Claudia thinks she's like the queen of etiquette or something. Anais goes on, "The truth is, most of the spas I work with are owned by some sort of larger corporation, so I'll meet the manager and maybe the CEO a few times, but it's not like this, where there's a great family who owns the place and really cares about every single detail."

"We're just the best," Mom says, staring at Anais's floor-to-ceiling window with the most unbelievable view of the beach. "Aren't we, guys?"

Everyone else in my family rolls their eyes at my mom, but at this moment I just want to run up and hug her. Maybe that's what we need—a little unity, a little family pride.

After our champagne toast and tour of Anais's apartment, where we debate which room has the best view of the ocean, we all head down to the beach. Anais suggested that we could watch from her balcony, but we have our traditions. The Desbergs do the Fourth of July the same way every year, and we can't change that.

Mom carries backpack beach chairs—she can carry three at once, and it's so impressive. Grandma brings a huge picnic blanket that folds up into a tiny square. And we have the best picnic food ever: sandwiches from the deli—turkey, mozzarella and tomato, grilled vegetables and Brie—and bags of potato chips and fresh-baked chocolate chip cookies. We always get to the fireworks a few hours early so we can get a good spot and enjoy our picnic without everyone stomping all over us looking for a spot.

The Ramals usually find us and put their blankets and

chairs near ours. When we were little, Sunny and I would pretend each of our blankets was a little island and if we stepped on the sand, we'd drown. So we'd hop from blanket to blanket.

It was such a silly game, but we had so much fun doing it. And sometimes we'd try to push Yamir off the blanket and pretend he was drowning.

I'd never do that now. Now I wish he'd sit with me on our blanket. I'd be so happy to have him there, but I'd never tell him that. I guess I could ask him, but he'd probably make a joke and embarrass me.

We set up our space. Bean arranges the chairs around the blanket, and Gary and Bevin bring a sushi boat as an appetizer. It's one of the really pretty ones too, with all the rolls arranged in a cool way and flowers made from the ginger. I don't know how they got it here still looking so perfect after a walk across the sand.

"Do you like sushi?" Bevin asks me. She pops a spicy tuna roll into her mouth. "It's my favorite."

I can't help but laugh because food is falling out of her mouth and she doesn't even seem to be embarrassed. I take a piece of yellowtail and scallion. "I love it too. And I'm so glad you got it from Sushi by Gari—it's the best in the area. They have locations in New York and Japan too."

"Really? Authentic!"

"Yeah, Gari bought a summer home here, so he opened another location." I smile, dipping a roll in soy sauce. "Lucky us."

Soon the Ramals find us, and set up their blanket and chairs. Sunny's mom always brings Indian food for their picnic and it always stresses me out. It's just so messy. The containers usually leak and Sunny usually ends up upset because there's dripping sauce on her leg.

Picnics are more fun when the food is easy to eat—sandwiches, sushi, stuff like that.

Actually, that's a rule I just thought of: Picnic food should start with *s*: sandwiches, sushi, soda, salsa, salami. And then I run out of other *s* words.

I turn away to grab a piece of tuna sushi and when I turn back around and look at the Ramals' blanket, I notice someone else is there with them.

"You're back?" I say, when Evan makes eye contact. "I thought you were in the Berkshires until the tenth."

He takes a piece of naan and dips it in the curry sauce. "I couldn't miss Old Mill Fourth of July! Are you crazy?"

He says that really loud and my whole family and the rest of the group turns around.

"No. I'm not crazy." I laugh. "Sunny said you were staying longer. That's all."

"I came back early," he says. "My uncle was driving back to Manhattan for work, so he gave me a lift."

"Oh." I force a smile.

"Want some of our chicken, Luce?" Sunny asks me.

"No, thanks. Too hot for me." I fan my mouth. "Temperature *and* spice!"

Bevin's the only one who laughs at my joke, but that's because she laughs at everything—and it's not just a laugh but a laugh and snort combination. It sounds so bad, it makes me not want to tell any more jokes.

Claudia is pretty much sitting in Bean's lap. Grandma and Anais are in some deep conversation about the history of Japan, Gary went to wash his hands somewhere, and Mom's reading an article on green living.

I turn back to the Ramals. Yamir hasn't even said hi to me yet, and now he's gone. Evan and Sunny are doing the slaps game where you have to move your hands away fast so the other person can't slap them.

I taught Sunny that game.

"I'll be right back, Bevin," I tell her because she's the only one who will notice that I'm even gone.

I still have a few hours until the fireworks start. It's only six, and they usually start around nine. It used to be that the hours before the fireworks were almost as much fun as the fireworks, but now it doesn't seem to be that way.

I walk across the beach and over to the carousel, and then I just keep walking. I don't know where I'm going, but I'm glad to have a break from everyone.

I keep walking, across the beach parking lot and through the neighborhood, and soon I'm in town, on Ocean Street, right near the pharmacy.

I have my own key, so I let myself in.

This is my family's store. My store. I'm allowed to be here. I have my own key and I know the alarm code. But even though I tell myself that, I still feel like I'm doing something I'm not supposed to be doing.

I go in and walk around the aisles, seeing if there's anything that needs straightening. But everything looks neat and tidy and perfect.

Now that Tory and Charise are back, Grandma doesn't even do her daily inspection of the aisles, giving me lists of what to work on. She knows the store will look perfect. Even the office is neat.

I wonder what Gary and Bevin have done to the upstairs apartment, but I know I can't go up and look. I'm sure they lock it anyway, and they have their own entrance at the back of the building, so they don't always have to walk through the store.

When I'm done inspecting the pharmacy, I go over to the spa.

The construction is nearly done. One of the treatment rooms has pink walls and one has green, and the entryway has pink and green stripes on the walls. The space where the reception area will be is all cleaned out and we're just waiting for the furniture to be delivered.

Toward the back there will be a rejuvenation area, where people can wait for their treatments. We'll have pitchers of water with fruit pieces floating in them and serene music playing. And we'll have robes that say PINK & GREEN on them. We'll have organic fruits if people get hungry, and the towels we're getting are made from some recycled materials.

At least I hope we will. That's how I envisioned all of this. But then I remember that envisioning something and something actually happening is really different. I feel like somehow I got off the path of planning the spa, and now I can't get back on.

It's strange how things can get off track so quickly. Like somehow I got replaced as Sunny's best friend, and somehow forgot how to act around Yamir, and somehow got replaced as Claudia's sidekick.

Somehow all of these things changed all at once, and now I don't know how to fix them.

I take one of the rolling desk chairs out of the interview room and roll myself through the spa area. Think, Lucy, think. I can do this. Because it's not enough to just have your own chair, you need to actually do something with that chair.

I look at my watch. It's already seven thirty. I'll stay here a half hour longer and then I'll go back to the beach. I don't want to wait too long or I'll never be able to make my way through the crowds to find our blanket.

As I'm rolling around the spa area, I notice that the high chair for hair and makeup is unpacked from its plastic wrapping. It's probably weird to say this, but this chair is beautiful. It's white porcelain with brass finishes, and the seat cushion is a navy blue corduroy. Mom, Grandma, and I picked it out as soon as we found out we got the grant and that Gary was investing.

It was one of the first things we did. And it was so much fun. We spent a whole Saturday night poring over the spa supplier catalogs Mom had ordered and we each picked out three chairs and then we narrowed down our choices and we voted.

It was unanimous. This was our chair.

It felt so real and exciting, like things were actually happening.

I quickly glance around just to make sure no one is looking in the window, and once I see that the coast is clear, I climb up in the chair, adjust the headrest, and sit back. From this high chair, I can see everything—the whole street, all the stores, people walking by. It's like a lighthouse in Old Mill, but my very own.

I look at my watch again. OK, it's almost eight. I really need to go back.

I'm climbing down from the chair backward (I've never been able to go down ladders facing front; I'm too much of a scaredy cat) when I hear sobs.

Uh-oh. I've been discovered.

I sneak around the chair and hide behind it. But the sobs keep getting louder, and then I realize I'm such a dummy because I've left all the lights on in the spa area. It's not even that dark out yet, I didn't need lights, but I left them on.

"Are, um, are—are—are you open?" I hear someone say through sobs. It sounds like a girl, but it could be a young boy. Bevin? I'm not really sure. I stay quiet. Maybe this person will just go away if no one answers.

"Hello? Anyone?"

I peek around the chair, but I still can't see the person. I have no idea what I should do. I'm not really supposed to work the cash register. Maybe I could convince the person to come back tomorrow to buy what they need. Only what if they have some sort of emergency?

I don't know what to do. But I need to be fast because I'm going to miss the fireworks.

"Hello?" the person says again, still sobbing.

"Hello!" I pop out from the chair like some kind of weird clown in one of those jack-in-the-box toys.

"Oh!" the lady screams. "I didn't see you there. Um, OK. Well, are you, um, open?" She's just standing there, sobbing, rubbing her eyes with the sleeve of her pale blue oxford shirt. She's thin with long blond hair and very short khaki shorts. She looks like a model, in a way. But a very sad model.

"Not really." I clench my teeth. "But I'm sure we'll have what you need tomorrow, if you come back then. OK?"

"You're not a spa?" She talks and cries at the same time. "I thought I read about you in the local paper, some interview with someone. Am I wrong? Oh, I'm so tired, I can't remember anything."

I pull over the other rolling chair and motion for her to take a seat. I don't know what else to do.

"No, you're right. We are a spa, but we're expanding, so we're not like officially open, but maybe I can help you anyway?" This lady looks so pathetic that I don't even know what to do. How can someone so pretty look so pathetic?

Finally she sits down in the chair and rests her face in her palms, and starts massaging her eyebrows, like she's trying to relieve the tension.

"OK." She pauses and takes a deep breath. "When will you be open?"

I can't help her if she doesn't tell me what's wrong. I wish she'd just tell me, but I don't want to pressure her. Also, I don't know how to explain to her that it's already after eight and I really need to get back to the beach for the fireworks.

Anyone and everyone in Old Mill and the surrounding towns knows about the Fourth of July fireworks. She must not be from here. She must be new.

There must be more to her story.

"We're opening officially Labor Day weekend—it's this huge weekend around here, called Boat Fest. Everyone has their boats out. There are street fairs, a carnival on the beach, amazing food. It's the best weekend ever." I smile and try to get her to smile too, but she still looks really, really sad.

"Labor Day weekend?" She perks up, finally.

I nod. "It's really not that far away. After the Fourth of July, it always seems like the summer is over, doesn't it?" I realize that was an idiotic thing to say. That it will only depress her more, and now I feel depressed too.

"OK." She's nodding slowly like she's figuring something out. She smiles at me, stands up, and walks over to the window. She takes her phone out of her pocket and hits a few buttons. She says into the phone, "I found a place. OK? But please don't treat me like that again." She pauses. "Mom, why do you have to do that? Don't you see it's my day?" She pauses again and keeps opening her mouth but not saying anything, like the person on the other end won't let her get a word in.

Finally, after a few more minutes of that, she hangs up.

"OK, I need to book you guys for the Saturday of Labor Day weekend. Eight bridesmaids, one bride, one mother of the bride, and one mother of the groom." She looks down at her phone again. "Makeup. Hair. Nails. Whatever else people do."

It occurs to me that this girl never goes to spas, never has her hair done, never does any of this.

"We can do that." I get her name, her number, and all of her info.

"Thank you so much," she says. "And your sign is amazing."

"Our sign?" I ask.

She walks outside and I follow her. "Yeah." She points up. "Your sign."

I hadn't even seen it yet. I came in the side door to the pharmacy, from the neighborhood, not through town.

But it's there. Our beautiful sign.

THE SPA AT OLD MILL PHARMACY

The PINK part is in pink and the GREEN part is in green, obviously, and it looks so beautiful and perfect and wonderful.

"You don't understand how glad I am that I found you," the girl says once we're back inside. "I don't even read the local paper ever, but I am so glad I did. My parents just bought a place here, and they're throwing the wedding for us in their yard, which is like ten acres, and they're being so impossible. Not letting Owen and me have a say in anything. And my mom is just . . ." She curls her lips inside and starts crying again. "She just can't understand it's not about her, and I know she's excited, but it's just so stressful."

I nod. "It'll be OK." I put a hand on her shoulder. I don't know what else to say. I mean, I could figure it out, but right now I really just want to see the fireworks.

I love helping people. And so I feel selfish for thinking this, but I need to see the fireworks.

"Hey, I have an idea!" I start turning off the lights in the spa. "Come with me to the fireworks! Do you know there are fireworks tonight?"

"I don't know anything." She shakes her head. "I just got in today. And the first thing my mom said was how disappointed in me she was that I hadn't booked a spa for the wedding."

I nod. This woman clearly feels the need to share all of her family's dirty laundry with me. And I love helping people with their problems, but not now. "OK, this will cheer you up! Come with me." I make sure all the lights are turned off, and the alarm is back on, and we leave the spa.

We're walking back to the beach with exactly fifteen minutes to spare. We may not make it back to my family's blanket, but we'll make it back to the benches on the boardwalk. And I'll text Claudia and say I ran into some people, so my family doesn't worry.

As we're walking, I realize that I just wrote down this girl's name for the appointments and I already forgot it. That's embarrassing.

"I'm so sorry, but your name just slipped my mind," I say. "I'm Lucy. Did I tell you that already?"

She laughs. "You did. But don't worry. I'm Sarabeth."

"Pretty name," I say.

We get back to the beach and I see immediately it's going to be hectic to get back to our blankets.

I text Claudia.

Ran into ppl from Hebrew school. see u after fireworks. Xo

84

I had to say Hebrew school because if I said regular school, Claudia would tell Sunny, Evan, and Yamir and they'd never believe me or they'd need to know who it was.

She texts back.

Have fun.

Sarabeth and I find a seat on the benches and we sit together and watch the fireworks.

It isn't at all how I expected to spend the Fourth of July, but it's good.

It seems like I'm on the right track to feeling like myself again.

Lucy's tip for a great summer:

Have as many picnics as you possibly can.

Lucy! Where have you been?" Mom yelps as soon as she sees me waiting by the car. The beach is walking distance from the pharmacy, but not from our house, and even if it were, there was no way we could've walked with all the chairs and food and stuff we brought.

"I texted Claudia." I shoot my sister a look, but she's too busy playing with Bean's hair to notice. "I ran into some people from Hebrew school. So we hung out by the benches and got some Dairy Queen."

I am totally planning on telling them about Sarabeth and all the business I just brought in for opening weekend, but now doesn't seem to be the time. Grandma and Gary are struggling to get all the chairs back in the trunk and Bevin is begging her dad for an ice cream. And Claudia is still playing with Bean's hair. Can't he just get a haircut already?

"Oh, but Sunny, Evan, and Yamir were with us," she says like she knows something's up. "Yamir even asked me where you were." There's a clump of sand on the pavement and she swishes it around with her shoe when she asks me that. She doesn't want to embarrass me; I can tell.

"Oh." I shrug. "Yeah, I ran into some other kids. They don't know them." My mom probably knows I'm lying since I'm not saying the other kids' names, but she doesn't push it.

Gary and Bevin take their car (an amazing convertible) back to the pharmacy apartment and the rest of us pile into our car. Mom and Grandma get the front, and then Bean, Claudia, and I sit in the back.

"Yamir looked really upset that you just disappeared, Luce," Claudia says, nudging me with her elbow. At least she's the one in the middle seat this time and I don't need to sit next to bony Bean.

I don't know what to say. If I act excited, Claudia will continue talking about it and embarrass me further. If I don't say anything, she'll ask me a million questions about what's going on.

"He was just trying to make conversation," I say finally. "I texted him and told him I was hanging out with some other people."

Claudia glares at me. "I don't think so. They didn't seem

to have any idea where you were. Even Sunny. Seems super-weird."

"Whatever, Claudia. You're super-weird for just bringing your boyfriend home and not telling anyone."

"Lucy!" Mom yells from the front seat. "Enough. Let's have quiet for the rest of the ride."

If I had a penny for every time I've heard my mom say that, I'd be rich. For real.

We get home and Grandma asks if any of us want a cup of tea. I say yes only because I know Mom will say yes and I want a chance to sit and talk with them about Sarabeth.

We all change into pajamas and settle in the den. Bean has Claudia's Old Mill High School sweatshirt on and it looks so bizarre on him. I wish he could just wear his own sweat-shirt, but apparently he borrowed it once and decided it was the most comfortable sweatshirt he'd ever worn. I wish every single thing he did didn't annoy me so much. He could end up being my brother-in-law one day, and I don't think it's good to hate your brother-in-law.

"Ah, another wonderful Fourth of July," Grandma says, putting her feet up on the leather ottoman. "There's something about the Fourth of July that feels empowering, isn't there?"

She looks at all of us.

"Well, if you're into that patriotic stuff," Mom says. "Truthfully, I'd like to see the Fourth of July become a day of service where we help those less fortunate in our communities."

I agree with what Mom's saying, but why can't we just leave a good thing alone for a minute? Fireworks, hot dogs, the beach. I mean, it's perfect as it is. Let's just enjoy it.

"Anyway," I say, trying to change the topic. "So, actually, I'm sorry to say this, but I lied."

Everyone gasps; Grandma gasps the loudest and covers her mouth. Sheesh. I can't even imagine what she thinks I'm about to say. Lying is a big no-no in our family, but still.

"No, not about anything crazy. I haven't, like, dropped out of school." I laugh, but no one else does, so I go on. "But I mean, I lied about tonight. I wasn't with some kids from Hebrew school."

"Shocking!" Claudia says, and rolls her eyes. I wonder where she thinks I was. I should've been putting up posters searching for a new sister!

I ignore her and turn to face Mom and Grandma, sitting together on the smaller couch. "I walked over to the pharmacy, just to clear my thoughts, and then a customer came in."

"Lucy, how many times have I asked you not to mess with the cash register?" Grandma says, all frustrated. No one in my family ever even gives me a chance to finish a sentence!

"I didn't use the cash register." I pause and wait for her to say something, and I can see her mouth opening to interrupt me again. "Will you please let me finish my story?"

They nod.

"Promise?"

"Just go on, Lucy," Claudia says.

Bean keeps burning his tongue on the tea and then making this ridiculous over-the-top expression. It's kind of funny but also distracting.

"So I was in the spa area, and this really frazzled woman came in. Her parents just bought this mansion summer home here, and that's where they're having the wedding, and this woman needed to find a place to do hair and makeup for her, the bridesmaids and the moms and everyone the day of the wedding."

"When's the wedding?" Bean asks. "Because my manicuring skills really aren't up to snuff yet."

Claudia hits him on the arm.

"Ow," he says, and then starts rubbing the spot.

"It's Labor Day weekend, Bean." I shoot eye-daggers at him. "So we have plenty of time. And that's our grand opening! And we have this huge wedding party! For hair and makeup."

I stand up and take a bow. "No applause. Thank you. No applause."

They laugh, but it sounds a little forced.

"That's really wonderful, Lucy," Grandma says. "I'm sorry I thought you were monkeying with the cash register. I'm glad you found these clients."

"Me too," I say. "So I didn't start telling her about how I do the makeup and everything. She seemed so frazzled and upset that I just booked the appointments and then we walked down to the beach and watched the fireworks together."

"Oh, very sweet," Mom says.

"Um, guys, I think we need to tell her," Claudia says to Mom and Grandma and then looks at me.

"Tell me what?" I ask.

"You know you're not going to be, like, the makeup artist at the spa?" Claudia says. "Right?"

"Well, I know you're hiring other people too," I say.

"OK." Claudia leans over and gives me a hug. "You're the cutest, Lucy-Luce."

People always have to say something like *you're so cute* right after they break some bad news. They must think that makes them sound nicer, but it doesn't.

I have to be allowed to do makeup, especially for my repeat customers like Kristin and Erin and Laura Gregory. That's how we got the idea to start a spa in the first place! But there's no point in arguing with them now. I have appointments booked for the next few weeks, so I'm just going to go ahead with them like nothing has changed. They'll see I'm needed on their own.

"Sarabeth is really great, though," I add.

Grandma says, "Let's make sure to tell Anais tomorrow. We want her to know about all appointments, especially the first ones, and we want her input in everything."

I nod.

"And we need to tell Gary too," Grandma adds. "Lucy, remember all of this, OK?"

"OK, will do," I say. "I'm gonna go to bed. I'm really tired."

"Night, sweetie," Mom says.

Claudia adds, "Night, Luce."

When I get upstairs, I check my cell phone.

I missed three text messages since coming home from the fireworks.

Two from Sunny:

U r so weird. Why did u disappear? On your fave night of the year?

Where r u? I am worried.

And then one from Yamir:

Didn't see u at fireworks. Skee-ball tomorrow?

I feel too tired and overwhelmed right now to respond to them. Sometimes it's just nice to know you were missed and to relish that feeling for a few minutes before you respond and acknowledge the people who were missing you.

I should be happy that Mom and Claudia and even Grandma were excited about Sarabeth being one of the first spa customers. But even with their excitement, it still didn't seem right. They just wanted me to make sure I told Anais and Gary. And then that whole thing about doing makeup was weird.

I feel like my emotions are a seesaw, and one minute I'm up and the next I'm down.

It's like those videos Mrs. Eldridge made us watch in health class about our changing moods. We all laughed about it at the time, but now I'm thinking they had some truth to them.

The next few days are super-busy.
Claudia told Anais all about the interviews, and they have
decided which beauticians they want to call back for a second round and for sample procedures.

Claudia volunteered to be the tester-person, which basically means that these cosmetologists will come in and do
sample procedures on her.

She'll be getting facials, waxing, her hair done, makeup,
everything.

"OK, I've printed up these checklists so, as the people
come in, you guys can be checking off the things that they
do well and the things they don't do as well," Anais says to
Bean and me. "But I need you to be honest, OK?"

"Sure," I respond. "But you know, I know a lot about

makeup. I think I could be a good tester-person. Can I please volunteer for at least one?"

Anais pulls me closer and whispers, "Lucy, if I let you do it, then I have to let Bevin do it, and Bevin's just not as mature as you are." She pats me on the back. "Please understand."

"Fine," I groan. But I don't really care about Bevin. Bevin should have a nanny who's taking her to the beach and the pool every day. She's bored at the spa. Right now she's playing some bowling game on Bean's iPad. She doesn't care at all about what's happening.

But I bet it will end up being so busy and hectic and Anais won't even notice when I hop up in the makeup chair. I'll find a way.

I walk over to the office to grab a Band-Aid out of the first-aid kit. These new flip-flops are cutting the skin on my toes where the rubber rubs against them.

"Well, when do you want to tell them?" I hear Mom say in the office, and then wait for Grandma's response. Tell us what? For a family who hates lying, there seem to a million secrets spiraling around here lately.

I wait a few seconds and I still don't hear Grandma's voice.

"Claudia might be heading back to school by then," Mom says. She's on the phone. Duh. Why don't I ever pick up on this? Probably because Mom hates talking on the phone. But she hates video-chatting even more because she says she's never "camera-ready."

"Because I don't know what Claudia's doing," Mom goes on. "She has her own life to lead. She's here now, but she could be gone tomorrow, for all I know. You know how it is when you're that age. She's free and she's enjoying her freedom."

Barf. I hate how it's always Claudia this and Claudia that. She basically has no rules to follow and they're all about "giving her space."

"OK, well, once you finalize everything . . ." Mom pauses. "And I mean *really* finalize, then we'll tell everyone." Silence again. "OK, right. Very good. Yes, OK. Take care."

Mom hangs up, and I knock on the office door, then walk in for a Band-Aid. "These flip-flops are killing me," I say. "How long will it take for me to wear them in?"

"I don't know, Luce," Mom says quietly, staring at the computer. "I'm late for a meeting at the *Old Mill Observer*. They want to talk about the grand opening and how everything's going. They have a special magazine section for the summer months, and I think we're going to be the cover story!"

"That's amazing!" I put on my Band-Aid and then wrap my arms around Mom's neck. "That is such awesome news. Can I come?"

She swivels around in her chair. "Luce, Anais needs you here."

I nod. Yeah, right. Everyone says everyone else needs me, but then when I think about it, I'm not sure anyone really needs me.

"Lucille!" Bevin's running through the pharmacy screaming. "Lucille! Lucille! Where *aarrreeee* you?"

Fine, maybe I was wrong. One person needs me. That person is Bevin. And I really wish she didn't.

"In here, in the office," I call back.

"I've been looking all over for you. Do you want to go see that new Princess Confidential movie? My dad said I could go. It's playing at one P.M."

My mom's still typing at her computer. Why can't she say that "Anais needs me" right now?

"I need to be here, Bevin. Sorry." I throw away the Band-Aid wrapper and leave the office. "Anais wants me to help evaluate the spa interviewees."

She follows me. "Oh. OK."

"Sorry. We can go see it later, maybe."

"Really? Oh, that's great! It's playing tonight too!" She claps. "I'm *soooo* excited. I've seen the first three. Have you?"

I don't have the heart to tell her that I only saw the first one and that's because it came out when I was in fifth grade and even then it seemed really babyish.

"So do you want to go to the six o'clock showing?" she asks.

"Um." I'm about to say yes and then I remember Yamir's text about Skee-ball. I really, really want to go down to the beach and play Skee-ball with Yamir and maybe get Frostees after. It sounds almost like a real date.

Then I keep imagining it, and instead of getting excited about the plan, I get nervous. I get that seeping-pit-of-lava feeling in my stomach.

I can't do that with Yamir. I like him. I really do. But being alone with him on the beach, at night, the moon shining over our heads, the sound of the waves hitting the shore . . .

It's all the things I love to do, but then rolled together and combined, it's scary. So scary that I want to run away. So scary that I'd rather go see that stupid princess movie with Bevin.

"Sure. That sounds perfect." I smile. "The interviews should be over by five, anyway."

"Yay!" Bevin yells, and then wraps her arms around me. "Movie buddies!"

"Yup," I say quietly, and pull out of her hug. "I need to find Anais and Claudia now. I think I hear the first candidate coming in."

"I'll come too," she says, and follows me to the spa area.

Wear sunscreen. You will still tan, but you won't burn.

So think of this as a sort of interactive interview," Anais tells Miranda, our first interviewee.

Miranda keeps shifting her weight from foot to foot and twirling the end of her hair. "OK, but I'm not completely familiar with these products, so would you mind just going over them with me?"

Anais scratches her forehead. "They're pretty standard. But sure."

Anais starts giving Miranda a tour of the spa area while explaining the products. Bean's unpacking boxes of supplies, and it's good to see him making himself useful. Bevin and I are just standing around because we need to observe this spa treatment that Miranda's going to do on Claudia. The longer I stand, the more nervous I get. This Miranda girl could have absolutely no idea what she's doing, and she's going to start treatments on my sister. If she doesn't know to shake out the towel, Claudia could have third-degree burns on her face! If she leaves the cold cream on too long, Claudia's face will completely break out. So many things could go wrong if you don't know what you're doing.

My mind immediately jumps to Courtney Adner and the hair trauma she had on homecoming, and how I felt so awesome the day I helped her fix her hair. I haven't seen Courtney around lately. I think she works as a counselor at summer camp. She was here toiletry shopping a few weeks ago. She spent forever in the pharmacy picking out what she needed. She said toiletries are her favorite thing to shop for, and I totally understood that.

"OK, we're ready," Anais says, a little out of breath, brushing her wispy curls away from her face. "Miranda, you'll be working on Claudia here." Anais puts a hand on Claudia's shoulder and Claudia smiles from ear to ear like she's some kind of model.

"What should I do?" I whisper in Anais's ear.

She looks down at her papers. "You'll be evaluating, Lucy, like I said before." For the first time, Anais sounds annoyed with me. "Here, Bevin, you take an evaluation sheet too." Anais rolls over the two office chairs and guides us to sit down.

I've never felt so useless in my whole entire life. Bevin doesn't know anything about these treatments, and so if she and I are filling out the same forms, those forms can't be important. Anais doesn't really need us evaluating. I bet my grandma said I need to be included, and so she found something harmless for me to do.

I shouldn't have insisted on this. Grandma and Mom said I could go to art camp at Connecticut College. They said I'd be busy with that and swimming and everything, but I told them I wanted to be around the spa as much as possible and spend as much time with Claudia as possible.

Yeah, right. It was all a mistake.

I uncap my roller-ball pen; at least Anais isn't forcing us to use golf pencils or something. That would make the situation way worse. I write Miranda's name at the top and start checking off the procedures she'll be doing.

I look up at Claudia on the fancy white table, lying perfectly flat, some kind of cold cream being spread on her face. I should be the one up there. I'm the one who knows all about spas and everything from all the research I did.

"Why do you look so upset, Lucille?" Bevin asks me, and grabs my arm like she's trying to be supportive.

"I'm fine." I force a closed-mouth smile.

"You don't look fine."

"Bevin. I'm fine."

"Fine." She cracks up even though nothing about this conversation has been funny. "I haven't seen Yamir around here lately. Did you guys break up?"

"Shhh. Miranda's trying to work." I point over in their direction and see Miranda struggling to get the cream off Claudia's face with some kind of washcloth. Doesn't she realize the washcloth needs to be wet? And it should be warm too. Even I know that.

"Did you guys break up?" Bevin asks again, whispering this time.

"No, we did not break up," I say through my teeth. "Now, shhh."

We sit here evaluating, but in almost every category, Miranda gets a "needs improvement" rating. She struggles with everything and when she finally finishes, she's dripping with sweat. You do not want your aesthetician to be sweaty.

"OK, well, thank you, Miranda," Anais says, shaking her hand. "We'll be in touch."

"When can I expect to hear from you?" Miranda asks.

"Um . . . within the next few weeks." Anais consults her clipboard, not making eye contact. "Thanks again."

Once Miranda's gone, Anais lets out her breath and plops down on the spa reception-area couch. It's such a nice couch that it's hard for me to believe it's ours. It's this beautiful brown velvet, kind of antique-looking.

Anais found it while she was antiquing in the Berkshires a few weekends ago, and she e-mailed us a picture and we all immediately approved. She had it shipped right away.

"So how did we all feel about Miranda?" Anais asks.

I look down at my sheet even though I don't need to. "She wasn't very good," I say.

"She didn't seem to know what she was doing," Bevin adds.

"Yeah, and um . . . ," Claudia starts, getting our attention. We all look up.

"Oh my gosh!" I scream. "Claudia! We need to get you to a hospital."

There are bright red splotches all over Claudia's face, kind of like she fell face-first into a forest of poison ivy. Some parts are even a dark burgundy-looking color, and one eye is starting to swell up. Miranda left the exfoliant on too long, and she probably didn't know to use one for sensitive skin!

"Claudia, come here please." Anais grabs her by the hand and leads her into the spa bathroom. She sits her down and starts blotting her face with witch hazel and dipping cloths into a cup of chamomile tea. "This will help."

It's not just that Anais is a spa consultant; she really knows what she's doing. That makes me feel a little bit better.

After Claudia's skin emergency, Mom, Grandma, Gary, and Anais go into a closed-door meeting in the pharmacy office.

Claudia's resting in the Relaxation Room with cold cloths all over her face and Bean is waiting on her like she's the Queen of England. He brings her drinks and candy and even goes down to the deli to get her favorite sandwich—Brie and apple slices.

"Bean is *soooo* cool," Bevin whispers to me as we're working in the pharmacy, fixing up the aisle with the pain relievers and cough medicine and stuff like that.

"Really?" I ask.

"Oh, totally," she says. "He's so good to your sister. And he's the kind of guy who can wear a necklace and not look dorky."

I peek around the corner and notice Bean's necklace. It's made of rope with beads on it. It looks dirty.

"Whatever," I mumble. I don't want to get into this with Bevin. What does she know about boys anyway?

We finish our work on the shelves and Mom, Grandma, Gary, and Anais come out of their closed-door meeting. It's already after five and Bevin and I should probably be heading to the movies soon.

I walk over and tap Claudia on the shoulder. "How's your face?"

"Fine. I was just falling asleep," she mumbles, and I know that's my cue to walk away. Claudia's very serious about her sleep.

"Let's go tell the adults that we're leaving for the movies," I say. "Otherwise they'll worry."

Bevin nods and skips over to the spa reception area. Everyone's sitting on the couch talking and sipping tea. It doesn't seem like they're working that hard, but since Grandma seems so happy, I decide not to worry about it.

I gauge my mood based on Grandma's a lot of the time. If she seems happy, then I feel happy.

"Bevin and I are going to the movies," I tell them. "Can we have twenty dollars for snacks?"

"Luce, just take candy from here, OK?" Mom says. "The movie theater is so overpriced."

"But we want popcorn," I whine.

"Fine, here's twenty dollars." Gary opens his wallet and hands Bevin the money.

I'm not proud of my whining, but if I'm not going to get treated like a grown-up, I may as well get treated like a spoiled kid.

"Luce-Juice!" I hear someone yelling as we're leaving the spa area. Only one person in the whole world calls me that, so I obviously know who it is.

What is he doing here?

"Luce-Juice!" he yells again, and I see Anais stand up and look around, not seeming happy about someone running through the store yelling.

Grandma goes back to the prescription counter to help some new customers. "Yamir, please, keep it down, OK?" She smiles, but I can tell she's a little annoyed.

"Lucy in the spa with Be-eh-vin," he sings when he sees us, creating a new twist on the song "Lucy in the Sky with Diamonds."

"Very funny, Yamir."

"I thought so." He raises his arms for a double high five, so I oblige him and then Bevin high-fives him too and cracks up.

"You ready?" he asks me.

"Huh?"

"Didn't you get my texts? Skee-ball competition at the beach tonight? I entered us. You're the best Skee-baller I know."

Suddenly it feels like there are clumps of cauliflower in my throat. I look over at Bevin, who has her eyebrows twisty, and she's still clutching the twenty dollars from her dad.

"We need to be there in twenty minutes, come on," he says. "I mean, I'm a speedy walker, but you can get slow sometimes." He laughs. "Kidding, kidding."

"Um, I didn't know that was officially confirmed," I say,

and then realize I sound like some kind of businesswoman. "So I, uh, made plans to see a movie with Bevin."

"Yup!" Bevin grabs my hand. "And we're gonna be late. Come on! We need to get popcorn and slushies and get good seats."

Instead of just the cauliflower lumpy feeling in my throat, now it feels like it's burning, like I swallowed a hot coal or something. I look over at Yamir and his eyes are scrunched and he's kind of frowning. It seems like hours of silence before anyone says anything.

"Oh, OK, no biggie," Yamir says finally. "Clint's free tonight. And he's really good at Skee-ball too. We'll win, for sure." He turns around and heads out of the spa area, toward the front of the pharmacy.

"Don't look so sad, Yamir!" Bevin yells.

I whack her in the arm. What is she thinking? She's yelling at Yamir right now, in front of everyone.

"Lucy likes you!" she yells, and I whack her again.

"Bevin!" I grab her arm to lead her out the back door. But she stands there, her feet firmly planted, like they were glued to the floor with rubber cement.

"Yamir! Are you listening? Lucy likes you! She really likes you!"

Now my family's out of the spa area and the Relaxation

Room and they're all standing in the doorway looking at me. Even customers are paying attention, popping up from the aisles. Every single person in Old Mill Pharmacy is staring at me right now.

It seems like Yamir is just going to walk right out without saying anything. I can't decide if I want him to say anything or if I don't. I guess I just want this moment to end. And I want to lock Bevin in her upstairs apartment for the rest of the summer.

"No time for that! I got a Skee-ball competition to win!" Yamir yells, with his back to us. "Later!"

I think I would have preferred if he had kept walking.

Now I'm standing there, feet stuck just like Bevin's. I don't know what to do. After a few seconds, the customers go back to their shopping. Claudia still has cold cloths on her eyes, but Bean leads her over to me like she's a blind woman and he's her Seeing Eye dog.

"Sorry, Luce," she whispers. "That was awkward."

"I know," I grumble.

"Bevin, may I have a word with you?" Claudia says, reaching out to grab her, since Claudia can't see a thing. Bean guides her over to Bevin and soon Bean is holding both of their hands, leading them into the Relaxation Room.

It's so ridiculous that it's funny, and I start to laugh. And then I start to cry. And then I'm laughing and crying at the same time. It reminds me of this song my mom wrote when she was in her acoustic-guitar-songwriting phase. She called it "How Can You Be Laughing When You're Crying?" It actually makes sense right now.

I overhear Claudia telling Bevin how wrong it was that she just did that, and Bean chimes in every few seconds, adding what he calls "the guy's perspective."

I plop down in the Turbo Massage Chair 7000 and turn on the massage button.

I bet Yamir will never talk to me again.

I'm missing the Skee-ball competition and I'll probably miss the movie too, not that I even wanted to see that dumb movie.

At least Claudia's looking out for me. That's one good thing.

Lucy's tip for becoming a better person:
Don't yell at anyone. Ever.

𝒲here did all of these makeup customers come from?" Grandma asks me, looking down at my appointment book as I'm setting up in one of the spa rooms. It occurred to me that I didn't need to keep doing makeup in the Relaxation Room now that the spa rooms are open. While I'm working, Anais, Gary, and Mom will be conducting a bunch more first-round interviews, since all the other candidates turned out to be horrendous.

"I had them scheduled," I tell her. "A few wedding trials, a few people getting their makeup done for that Connecticut Parks gala tonight."

Grandma nods. "That's great. Tell Anais so she knows and can greet people appropriately."

I sigh. "Grams, it's the same as it was before. They know I'm doing it. They made the appointments with me."

Grandma hugs me. "I know, I know, but we're a real-life spa now, and I want to make sure we're doing everything right." She pulls back from the hug and kisses me on the cheek. "We're a real-life spa because you made us a real-life spa."

"Oh, Grams." I roll my eyes.

I don't get why she's so concerned with Anais. But I find her and tell her, and she says, "Oh, lovely. Let me make sure the water pitcher is out and the tea, so we can offer them stuff when they come in."

"Good idea."

It's so hot today that I turn the air-conditioning to sixty degrees and even put on the ceiling fan. You cannot have it so hot while doing makeup, or all the makeup will melt on the person's face and then drip down. It can be pretty disgusting.

I was a little concerned that Bevin might show up today, but so far I haven't seen her. After she blurted out everything to Yamir, I can't trust her at all, and especially not around clients.

As I'm waiting for my first customer, I adjust the lighting in the room and arrange all of the makeup on the silver makeup table. It feels so amazing to have these incredible supplies. The brushes are brand-new and perfect. The table is just the right height and there are so many light combinations, depending on the natural light and how the person's sitting.

Anais runs out to the grocery store around the corner and

picks up fresh flowers for the vase on the reception room table. She puts out the beautiful glass pitcher (it's from Tiffany's; she got it at an estate sale, and it was still bubble-wrapped!) and fills it with water and fruit slices.

Even though we're still weeks off from the grand opening, there's something about today that feels so important, so special. My first time doing makeup in the spa area! And it all looks so beautiful.

Anais takes a seat behind the reception desk and keeps looking at her watch.

"You have an interview soon, right?"

"I do." She smiles. "I think we'll work in the pharmacy office since you're in there today."

"I'm just in one treatment room," I tell her. "You can still use the spa office and the other rooms."

She nods. "OK. Thanks, Lucy."

Anais is wearing a pale pink linen dress, and she looks prettier than ever. Her hair is in a low bun and as I peek over her shoulder, I notice her writing something in the most beautiful handwriting I've ever seen, curly and straight up and down, and perfect.

I want her to like me. I want her to be impressed with me. But it seems like the more we work together, the more annoyed with me she gets.

It feels like she just wants me to disappear.

"Hello, I'm Bella. I have a ten o'clock interview," a woman says, walking in. Anais stands up to shake her hand and leads her to the pharmacy office.

"I'll be right with you," Anais says.

A few minutes later, my makeup appointment arrives.

"Hi, Tessa!" I say, walking over to her. She's on the board of the Connecticut Parks Association and she's the MC for the gala tonight. We had a whole long talk about the event over the phone when the date for the gala was set back in April.

"Lucy!" She hugs me.

"Hello, welcome," Anais says after we break our hug. "Would you care for some water? Tea?"

"I'd love some water, thanks," Tessa says. And then I'm just standing there, suddenly doing nothing.

Anais and Tessa start talking about local businesses going green, and Anais says, "We hope you enjoy your time at Pink and Green. Lucy's helping out for now, but in September, after the grand opening, we'll be fully staffed."

I look at Tessa, but she doesn't make eye contact with me. She's nodding at Anais and sipping her water.

I can't believe she just said that. Doesn't she realize that I was the one who scheduled Tessa's appointment? Now I know for sure what Anais thinks about me. I'm just here for the meantime. I'll be replaced eventually. She hasn't even seen what I can do yet.

When I first met Anais, I thought she was perfect, someone I really wanted to be like. Now I'm not so sure what's going on. But I can't let my bad mood affect my makeup treatment. Tessa came here expecting the best, and she will get better than the best. That's one thing I know I can control.

After Tessa finishes her water and her long chat with Anais, I guide her over to the treatment room. She hops up in the chair and puts her head back and I flick the switch to turn on the serene music. Claudia and I sampled all of these albums to find the perfect ones to play in the spa.

I used to play music while I did makeup in the Relaxation Room, but it was on this old boom box with a CD player and sometimes the tracks would skip, which didn't make for a very relaxing soundtrack.

I'm cleaning Tessa's face with a warm washcloth and I'm wondering if she's going to bring up anything about what Anais said about the real staff coming after the grand opening. Tessa called me after her neighbor told her about Old Mill Pharmacy and my amazing makeup work. Tessa knows all about the pharmacy and the grant and the spa opening. I kind of want her to say something, or ask me about what

Anais said so I can explain, or so I can feel better knowing that someone else realizes Anais is wrong.

But so far, she's been quiet with her eyes closed. She seems so relaxed, I don't want to disturb her. Maybe she'll say something when I'm done and she sees how great she looks.

I'm priming her face with cold cream and then I'll do a light foundation. I let the cold cream settle for a second and quickly glance at all the makeup on the tray so I can map it out in my mind. And that's when I hear someone calling me.

"Lucille! Lucille!"

Uh-oh. I thought Bevin was out for the day.

I'm wiping off the cold cream with a warm washcloth when the door to the treatment room slams open and Bevin barges through. "Lucille! I was worried sick. I thought something happened to you."

I quickly whisper in Bevin's ear, "I'm with a client. Can we please discuss whatever you need a little later on?"

She covers her mouth and then cracks up. "Come on. I know you think you're like a makeup artist or whatever, but you're just a kid like me."

Tessa's being really polite, just lying there, looking relaxed. But I bet this little back-and-forth between Bevin and me is starting to get annoying, and she doesn't want to wait all day to get her makeup done. I don't know how much longer she'll stay polite.

"Bevin, please leave."

She rolls her eyes. "I can do makeup just like you. I swear. Let me help!"

I bite the inside of my bottom lip; I don't know what to do. I can't let her help, but I also can't get into a fight in front of a customer. Grandma says that's a big no-no. It looks totally unprofessional.

"Just sit." I guide Bevin over to the chair in the corner. It's really there for customers to put their clothes and bags on, but in this case Tessa hung everything up on one of the hooks behind the door. I knew those hooks were a good idea.

"I can help. Really!" Bevin whispers.

I ignore her and go back to Tessa. I start dabbing on the foundation and carefully blending it. "What time is the gala?" I ask her.

"It starts at six," she says softly, definitely the tone of a relaxed person, so that's good. "But I need to be there at four thirty for pictures and chatting with the press and all of that."

I look at the fancy clock above the door. It's just about three, so we have plenty of time. The gala is at the nature conservancy ten minutes from here.

"OK, I just want to make sure none of your makeup melts. It's almost a hundred degrees today. Can you believe it?"

She shakes her head. "Too hot. When I was younger, summers in Connecticut, especially by the shoreline, were very cool. Some people didn't even have air-conditioning. Now, forget about it. You'd never survive."

After I'm done dabbing on the foundation, I get started on her eye makeup. She wants a very subtle look and I have the perfect color combination for her. I have a pale gray for the base of the eyelids and then a lighter color for the creases. And I've really mastered my skill at gel eyeliner.

"OK, can I at least do the blush and lipstick? Please?" Bevin walks over to us. Tessa keeps her eyes closed. I'm really not sure what she makes of this situation.

"Bevin," I say through my teeth. "Not now."

She keeps standing there while I'm finishing Tessa's eyes. Then I turn away for a second to put down the eye makeup and assess what I want to do for her lips. And that's when Bevin swoops in.

By the time I'm turned back to face Tessa, Bevin is brushing on some blush round and round in circles on her cheeks. "Bevin!" I yell. "Cheekbones! What are you doing?"

She waves me off. Tessa sits up for a second and looks at me, and I make an it's-all-going-to-be-OK face. I guess she believes me, because she lies back down.

"Voilà!" Bevin says a few seconds later, holding up a hand mirror for Tessa.

"You didn't do lips yet," I whisper. "Lips are the finishing touch."

"I know, but I wanted her to see a work in progress."

I've been looking at Bevin this whole time and I haven't gotten a good look at Tessa. So when she sits up, I see what Tessa is about to see in about three seconds.

Horror. She looks like she's in some kind of horror movie. And the worst part of it is that the awful blush work totally negates the wonders I did on Tessa's eyes.

"Uh, um," Tessa says, looking at herself in the mirror.

I stare at Bevin. Does she really think she did good work here? How did I let her do this? It's all my fault.

"I can fix it," I tell Tessa. "Just give me five minutes. I still have to do your lips."

"You hate it?" Bevin asks.

Tessa looks at me and then at Bevin and then back at me. "I have to go, girls. Thanks." She forces a smile. "I usually like to do my own lips anyway."

Tessa gets up, grabs her stuff, and leaves the spa area. I walk out too, leaving Bevin alone in the treatment room. I can't even look at her right now. That's how mad I am.

As Tessa's leaving the store, I hear her on the phone. "Can I get a rush appointment? Just makeup?"

Sheesh. She couldn't have waited to make that call until after she left the spa? I guess she didn't have time to waste.

"Why did Tessa look so upset when she left the spa?" Anais asks me, catching me totally off guard.

"Uh, she did?" I ask. I have no idea how to play this. I feel like any second, a bucket of water is going to fall on my head.

Anais nods. "Lucy, did something happen?"

Suddenly I feel like there was some kind of hidden camera in that spa room, and they were all spying on me that whole time. Could that be possible? I am so paranoid.

"It's not my fault, Anais." I start sniffling and then before I know it, I'm all-out crying. Anais leads me into the Relaxation Room and sits down next to me on the couch. "Bevin barged in, and then grabbed makeup off the tray while my back was turned. And she totally ruined Tessa's makeup. It needed to be redone."

"Lucy," Anais says in that stern tone that teachers use. "If you are going to be a responsible part of the spa staff, then you need to know how to handle these matters."

I look up at Anais. She seems about as comforting as a cold metal pipe. Why doesn't she care how upset I am?

"You can't be blaming others. OK?"

I start crying even harder, but Anais still doesn't really do much to comfort me.

"This is a place of business, and if we want to be taken seriously, we need to act professionally." She pauses. "I know it's your family's place and you've been able to do whatever you want around here, but we really want to up the ante on the spa end of things."

Anais pats me awkwardly on the shoulder and leaves the Relaxation Room. I want to go complain to Mom or Grandma, but that probably won't help me.

I want to yell at Bevin, but I doubt that will help me.

I sit down on the Turbo Massage Chair 7000 to process my thoughts. I have one more makeup appointment today and a few more this week. I turn on the massage settings and lean back and try to relax.

And that's when it hits me: Yelling at Bevin won't help. Complaining that I'm not involved in the spa won't help either. Yamir said I complain too much, and maybe I do. But there is one positive way I can help, and actually make a difference.

The ultimate makeover: Bevin.

She's a total disaster: She says things she shouldn't, she ruins makeup, her shoelaces are always untied, she gets food stuck in the corners of her mouth. She tries really hard, but she just needs some guidance.

I can be that guidance. I can show her how to act better in public, how to do makeup, how to be a good friend.

If I can't make a difference at the spa, I can make a difference in one person's life. I can give Bevin a makeover, but not just makeup and hair and whatever else I used to do around here. I can do more than that. A personal-improvement makeover.

The more I think about this, the more excited I get. I can hardly wait another second. I need to find Bevin. I need to start helping her. But I need to do it in the perfect way, so it's not too obvious, so she doesn't think it's weird and back away from me.

This is going to be my new project.

I've heard people say that if you save a life, you save the whole world. So does that mean that if you give one person a makeover, you make over the whole world too?

I think so. It sounds good, anyway.

Lucy's tip for a great summer:

Barbecue as often as you can. It doesn't need to be fancy. But you will need hot dogs. Otherwise, it's not a barbecue.

If I had looked at the Earth Club meeting schedule more closely, I would have made sure to return Yamir's text about that Skee-ball competition. Because as my luck would have it, we have an Earth Club meeting only a few days after Bevin's blurting-out episode, and now I actually have to see Yamir face-to-face.

I thought I'd be able to avoid him for a while since Sunny's at Indian Dance Camp this week, but I guess not. Now I have to go to Earth Club without Sunny to help me.

"That's gonna be so awkward," Bevin says to me as I'm getting ready to leave. "Though I said what I said for a reason. I thought he needed to know, because like he kind of ignores you most of the time, and he should treat you better."

This is my moment. This is the beginning of the make-over.

"Bevin, here's the thing," I say in my most gentle voice, patting the chair for her to sit down. "Sometimes we say things that need to be said, because we think they need to be said, but the truth is, if we think a moment before we say them, we realize it's best to stay quiet." I pause. "Do you understand?"

Her eyebrows are crinkled. She doesn't get it.

"Sorry." She puts her head down on the desk. "No one even wants me here."

Ugh. Now I need to cheer her up. I can't just let her go around feeling terrible and not needed. This is the first step to helping her.

"Bevin," I say. "Come on."

She keeps sitting there, with her head on the desk, her dirty-blondish hair spread around her like some kind of old-fashioned fan.

"It's true. I know you didn't want me here. Even my dad is too busy for me. He thought I would be with my mom, but she had to do some photography expedition in Senegal."

It's kind of hard to hear her because her head's down on the desk. If Anais sees this, she will not be pleased. I should tell her I understand about dads being too busy and dads moving away and all of that. But sometimes it's hard to admit you're suffering too. It's opening yourself up, knowing you'll never be able to close yourself again.

"And now I messed things up with you and your boyfriend."

"Bevin," I say again. "I don't even know if he's my boyfriend."

Her head jerks up. "See! Exactly why I had to say something. You don't even know. And you want him to be. And you're just letting the whole summer—the most romantic time of the year—pass by without knowing or not!"

"OK, Bevin." I fold my hands in my lap. "How would you like to spend the afternoon together?"

"I thought you had Earth Club," she says.

"It's optional." I smile. "And remember the other day when you were complimenting me on my clothes and I said how it's all about having staple items in your wardrobe?"

She nods.

"Well, I have an idea. Let's go shopping. We'll find you a few new things. We'll have lunch. We can even meet up with some friends of mine."

Her eyes bulge and she starts clapping. "Really? Really? Really? You mean that?"

"Shh." I put a finger to my lips. "I don't need everyone knowing I'm skipping Earth Club."

"Oh-kay," she mouths.

Claudia pops her head in after the interview she's conducting ends. "Ready, Luce?"

"Yup." I hop up from my chair and motion for Bevin to get up too. "Bevin's coming also. We're actually going to the mall for the Earth Club meeting today."

"Huh?" Claudia makes a face.

"Yup. We're making sure the food court is recycling all glass and plastic bottles." I look over at Bevin to make sure she stays quiet. Yes, it's a total lie, but it actually sounds like a good Earth Club project. I make a mental note to tell Mrs. Deleccio about it later.

Claudia and Bean drop us off at the mall's main entrance and I quickly look around to see if there's anyone I know nearby.

I'm half wishing that there is, and half wishing that there isn't.

Claudia waves good-bye as she drives away and then it's just Bevin and me.

I take a deep breath. This is really happening. A whole day alone with Bevin, working on her personality-improvement makeover.

"What should we do first?" she asks.

"Are you thirsty?" I ask her.

She shrugs. "I guess."

"Iced tea!" We walk through the mall to the food court and stop at the Beverage Bodega. It's a stand that only sells beverages—everything you can think of: milk shakes, coffee, soda, smoothies.

"When meeting new people, it's good to have a beverage in your hand," I tell Bevin. "That way if you can't think of something to say, you can take a sip while you think of it."

She nods.

"And this iced tea is so delicious, isn't it?"

"Best iced tea I've ever had." She smiles, and then slurps her drink loudly, gulping it all down and finishing with a huge burp.

My first instinct is to get all frustrated and yell at her, but that won't help. "You finished it in three seconds. Try to savor it. And also, maybe you don't want to burp so loud. In the future, take little sips, and make it last longer."

"OK," she says, and looks down at her feet. Her shoelaces are untied and one sock is higher than the other, like always. It's going to be a long day. "Lucy, why are you suddenly, like, hanging out with me and telling me all this stuff? Did my dad pay you to spend time with me or something?"

I laugh and then cover my mouth. "No!"

"Well, then, why?"

I sigh, take a sip of iced tea, and say, "Well, here's the thing, Bevin. I was lucky enough to have Claudia as my older sister to guide me through life. And you don't have an older sister. And since I'm three days older than you, I decided that because you're in Connecticut for the summer, I can at least provide you with a little big-sister guidance."

She sniffles, then reaches over to hug me. She hugs me so tight, I can't move, and here we are standing right in the middle of the food court hugging for what seems like three years. Finally she lets go.

"That is so nice, Lucy."

We spend the rest of the day shopping and picking up what I like to call *staples*: plain tees and capri pants and hoodies and little white sports socks that will always stay put.

"You have a lot of nice stuff," I tell Bevin while we're on line to pay. "But you just need things that go with everything else, so you can change it up sometimes. And also you need new socks."

She looks down at her feet and laughs. "Yeah, this isn't even a matching pair."

"I could tell."

By the time we're done shopping, it's too late to meet up with people, so I decide socializing Bevin will be our next project.

And the truth is, I'm not really sure who I could introduce her to, since Sunny's away and even when she's here, she's always busy with Evan, and everything is so awkward with Yamir and me.

I'm going to need to find temporary friends during this makeover process.

Later that night, my mind races with ways I can help Bevin, and I can't fall asleep. I decide that since I'm awake I can do some more research for Earth Club. I feel a little guilty that I bailed on the last meeting just to avoid Yamir.

As I'm researching, I come across all these Going Green community groups. They're basically groups of people who meet every month or so to discuss their Going Green progress. And then I come across all these other groups—restaurant owners' groups, gardeners' groups, vegan groups.

There's basically a group for anything and everything.

It's kind of amazing that the Internet can bring people together. I bet before the Internet, these people just had to do their own thing and worry about problems on their own. Maybe they knew a few people here or there and discussed issues with them. But they didn't have this wide-reaching support system, and now they do.

I wonder if there's an eco-spa owners' group!

If I found a group to join, it would be the perfect way to show Anais and Gary and Mom and Grandma that I know what I'm doing, that I'm really a part of things and an important member of the team.

I keep looking up eco-spa owners, spa owners' groups, small business owners, new business owners, all kinds of things, and then I narrow it down to Connecticut. It wouldn't make much sense to join a group in California, even though it would be kind of fun to go there!

I think I'm getting closer when I stumble upon a message board with business owners from the Newport area. That's only about an hour from here. Some of them talk about spas and salons, and they're going through a lot of the same issues we are.

More research leads me to discover that there's a southeastern Connecticut and Rhode Island small business owners' group that is actually meeting a few times this summer! The next meeting is pretty soon, and it's not even far away. It's at the Bayberry Cove Library.

Their website says they're a support group for people opening new businesses or expanding old ones. They share tips and advice on all sorts of issues that come up. I have to go. Grandma's too busy, and Mom wouldn't be interested. It's up to me.

This group might know things we don't about how to open a new business—they certainly know more than I know! But if I go, I could start to feel like I know what's going on. I could have something to contribute.

Plus, if I'm going to be a spa consultant when I grow up, it couldn't hurt to get started now.

I'm about to write in and say that I'll be coming, when I realize that these people could probably get arrested for talking to a thirteen-year-old online. We had this whole seminar about that in school this year. There are all kinds of cyber rules, and I really don't want to get these innocent people in trouble.

So I don't respond. I just e-mail myself the meeting time and some other information. There's no age requirement for a meeting like this. It's at a library and anyone can be at a library.

I'm so excited that I found this that I have even more trouble falling asleep.

Lucy's tip for becoming a better person:
Compliment others as often as you can.

A few days later I'm at the kitchen table thinking about how much Bevin has improved already. Her socks always match, her hair is neat, she wears the clear lip gloss I gave her, and she hasn't blurted out anything inappropriate since the Yamir incident.

I hate to be conceited, but it could be my influence. She's getting positive attention from me and it's going a long way.

We were hanging out at the mall food court the other day and we ran into some kids from Hebrew school. She was totally normal around them—for the most part. I mean, she did ask Elon Rosenberg ten times what his name was because she kept forgetting, but he seemed pretty understanding about it. I think she has a crush on him, but she hasn't mentioned it yet.

She only tripped once, and in all fairness, it was because

this guy left his tray on the floor next to the garbage can instead of putting it on the dirty-dishes cart.

She's really improving.

I'm feeling pretty pleased with myself and all of my hard work with Bevin as I sip Mom's fresh-squeezed OJ. And then my mom puts down the *New York Times* and stares at me.

"Lucy, I have to talk to you," she says. "It's about Dad."

My throat immediately tightens up. My feelings about my dad are always wobbly like a seesaw. I used to secretly wish every night before bed that he'd come back. Then, over time, I sort of just stopped wishing for that. We had a great time when we were together, and life was pretty OK when we were apart too. But sometimes I can miss him really bad, with no warning. And then I get mad at myself for missing him and wishing he'd come back. He left us, and we're fine without him, really. Plus, I don't want to wish for something that may never happen.

We never really talked about it, though. Until now.

"Is he sick? What's going on?"

My mom seems relatively calm. So why does she make everything sound so dramatic?

"He's fine, he's fine." She laughs, but it sounds a little forced. "I know you and Claudia have been wondering when he's coming this summer, and it's been up in the air."

I gulp the rest of the juice. "We know that."

"Right." She goes into the pantry and takes out a brown bag that's greasy on the sides. "Chocolate croissants." She puts the bag on the table and gives me one and takes one for herself. Since this is pretty much our second breakfast, she must be breaking some kind of bad news. "His contract with Oxford is still being worked out, and he doesn't have the time this year for his regular two-week stay."

See? Breaking bad news.

But at least I get a chocolate croissant.

"So when is he coming?" I ask after a bite.

"Well," she starts, and then picks a few pieces off hers. "Remember our friend Esme? She's the one who went backpacking across Africa and brought you back that handmade doll?"

"Yeah. I know. The wedding. You already discussed this, remember?" I don't mean to sound rude, but Mom can get lost on a tangent forever, and I don't understand what this has to do with Dad coming to Connecticut.

"Oh, right. So yeah, your dad wants to come for the wedding, and then he'll take you and Claudia somewhere for a few days either before or after. So you will get to see him."

She smiles and it seems like there's more to the story, stuff she's not telling me, but I can't figure out what it is. It's almost a mischievous smile, the kind of smile Claudia has when she's getting away with something she shouldn't. She had this smile when she told us Bean was staying for the summer.

"OK, so what's the big deal?" I ask.

"No big deal, I just wanted you to know." She looks down at her plate, but she's still got that smile.

As I'm putting the dishes in the dishwasher, it occurs to me that Mom is thinking something she's not saying. She's terrible at keeping secrets. And it seems like Dad is just squeezing in his visit with us because he's going to this wedding. I don't want to be a squeeze-in. I want to be a priority.

Grandma, Claudia, and Bean are already at the pharmacy. Mom goes down to do the laundry, and then when she's done we'll be heading over there too. I try to come up with a game plan for Bevin and me for the day, but I can't focus. I find myself wandering from room to room looking for something to do.

I decide to e-mail my dad. Maybe I just need to show him that I want to be a priority! I need to take action.

Dear Dad,

Mom said you're coming for Esme's wedding. That should be fun. I have ideas for our getaway. Maybe we can go to Cape Cod? Or Nantucket? People always say how amazing Nantucket is. Or we could even go to Fire

Island. My Earth Club teacher just went and it's so awesome. No cars! Let's come up with an awesome plan. You'll have to ask Claudia if Bean (her boyfriend) is coming. No, that's not his real name. Claudia will explain. Anyway, miss you! I'm excited for your visit.
Lots of love,
Lucy

A minute later, I get a reply.

Lucy dearest!
Fire Island sounds great. I knew you'd have a plan. The dates for my trip are still up in the air. I'll e-mail you my itinerary as soon as I have it. Do you like Bean? If you like him, I like him. But I love YOU! Let's Skype this week.
Dad

It's a short e-mail, but it does make me feel a little bit better. He replied quickly and he's excited about my plan. At least there's someone in this family who cares what I have to say!

Lucy's tip for a great summer:
Wear flip-flops every day.
Try not to ever wear real shoes.

Bevin's waiting for me in the Relaxation Room. She's wearing the jean shorts we bought on our first shopping trip and a ribbed black tank top. She has her white Converse on with the little ankle socks.

She looks perfect.

"Hi, Luce," she says. I notice right away that she's stopped calling me Lucille. The training is working. She gets it.

I sit down next to her and notice Bean and Claudia walking someone out of the spa area. It seems like I haven't seen them in days—they're always so busy working on things and not telling me what they're doing.

Whatever. I don't need them. I have my own project, and it's actually more important. I'm helping Bevin. When she gets back to school in September, no one will even recognize her, and they'll all be so amazed at how much she matured over the summer.

"So what are we doing today?" she asks me.

"That's a good question." I sit back on the couch and try to think of something. I need to start introducing Bevin to people. Hanging out with the Hebrew school kids was fine, but I don't know them well enough to hang out with them all the time. And hanging out with me alone isn't going to help her much when she gets back to school in the fall. But Sunny is going to a minor league baseball game with Evan and his friends. I think Yamir is going too. And truthfully, I'm not sure it would be a good idea for Bevin to hang out with them again anyway, after her blurting-out episode. She's better, but she's not perfect yet.

I try to think about where other people from school hang out in the summer. A lot of kids are away at camp, but I'm not really friends with those people anyway.

Then I remember Annabelle Wilson and her friends, and how they love to hang out on the boardwalk, get hot dogs for lunch at Hotdogger & Co., and try to sneak into the rooftop pool at the Allegria.

They call themselves AGE because their names are Annabelle, Georgina, and Eve. And they are so totally obnoxious, but they're perfect for Bevin's training! Georgina is the only one in the group that I like. But she's the kind of girl that everyone in every group likes.

"Go get a bathing suit, and meet me in front of the spa area," I tell her.

"Should I change now?" she asks.

"No, just bring flip-flops, a bathing suit, and sunscreen in a bag."

I run into the pharmacy office to find my bathing suit. Ever since I was little, I always kept an extra bathing suit at the pharmacy. You never know when you're going to take a spontaneous trip to the beach. It's just the way things work around here.

My mom and Anais are on speakerphone arguing with someone about their inspection forms, and Grandma's ordering supplies online. I try to be as quiet as possible, shuffling through the desk drawers looking for my bathing suit, but everyone shushes me anyway.

And the bathing suit is nowhere to be found.

There's only one thing I can do.

I tiptoe up the stairs to Bevin's apartment and knock on the door. Bevin comes out with a gym bag slung over her shoulder.

"Bevin, I'm so sorry to do this, but can I borrow one of the bathing suits we bought at the mall the other day?" I ask her in my nicest voice.

"You want to borrow something of mine?" She sounds shocked.

"I can't find my bathing suit." I shrug. "And there's no time to go back to my house and get a new one now, and there's no one to give us a ride. And those suits we bought you are really cute."

She's nodding really fast. "Sure! I'm wearing the pink one, but you can wear the turquoise-striped one."

"Thank you so much!" I don't need to worry about flip-flops since they're the only shoes I wear all summer long, and we can steal towels from the spa supply closet. Mom made a mistake with the ordering and they were final sale, so we have way more than we need anyway.

We walk over to the beach. It's hot, but there's a nice breeze and little humidity, so we're not sweating that much. That's a good thing. It's never good to be super sweaty when meeting new people.

On the way over, I tell Bevin that we'll probably see my friends from school there.

"Sunny?" she asks.

"No, Sunny has plans, but other people," I tell her. "So

just be chatty and friendly. If you see them picking at their nails, or looking off into the distance, it means you're talking too much."

"Really?" She seems more fascinated by this than insulted, so that's a good thing. I don't want to hurt her feelings, but I do have to be honest. Sometimes she really goes on and on forever.

Just as I suspected, the AGE girls are sitting on one of the benches, drinking sodas, with towels draped over their shoulders.

"Lucy!" Annabelle calls out. I've known her since nursery school, but we've never really been friends. She's perfect for Bevin's training.

"Hi guys, this is my family friend Bevin." I gently push her toward them, and she waves and says hi. "Her dad is helping with the opening of the spa, so they're staying in Connecticut for the summer."

"Oh, cool," Georgina says. "Where are you from?"

"Manhattan," Bevin tells them, and then looks at me. I guess she's worried about talking too much, but she can say more than one word.

"Really?" Eve yelps. She's the shortest person I know and has a really high-pitched squeaky voice. "That is *sooooo* cool."

"Yeah," Georgina adds. "You, like, live in the best city in the world."

"I guess." Bevin laughs. "It's not like I hang out with celebrities or anything."

"Not even a Real Housewife?" Annabelle laughs.

"Not really." Bevin shifts from foot to foot and I try as hard as I can to think of something else to say, a conversation Bevin can participate in, so we're not just standing here awkwardly.

"I'm gonna go get us a snack," I tell Bevin. Maybe it's too soon to leave her on her own with people she doesn't know, but it might be good for her to jump right in. Besides, I'm a little hungry, and sharing snacks always helps cover awkward silences.

I get an order of onion rings and some cut-up watermelon and figure it should hold us over until lunch.

When I get back, Bevin's sitting on the bench between Georgina and Annabelle. They don't even notice me standing there.

"Would you rather eat only lima beans and chocolate for the rest of your life or get to eat whatever you want but no chocolate for the rest of your life?" Annabelle asks.

"That's kind of a weird one," Georgina says.

"I'd have to say the second choice," Bevin adds.

"Can I exchange lima beans for asparagus, because I *looooove* asparagus?" Eve asks.

"This isn't even your question," Annabelle says to her. "And obviously not!"

This goes on and on for about five more minutes, and then they notice me.

"Bevin's really good at *Would you rather*," Annabelle says, grabbing an onion ring from me.

"That's why I brought her to hang out," I tell them. "I knew you'd appreciate her skills."

Bevin smiles and sits up straighter. It's the happiest I've ever seen the girl, and I've known her for a while.

We stay at the beach for the rest of the afternoon. AGE embraced Bevin much quicker than I thought they would, so I don't have much to do. But I can't complain—that was my goal in the first place.

At five P.M., I get a text from Sunny.

Where r u? stopped by pharmacy. Gma said u were wit bevin?

I decide to ignore it. The whole story's too long to explain over a text and I really can't sneak away and call her right now anyway.

"Are you guys staying for the hot-dog-eating contest?" Georgina asks.

"I totally forgot about that!" I yell, and then remember that Sunny and Evan had mentioned something about it earlier. Back when we all hung out.

"Let's stay," Bevin says, a whine in her voice like a little kid. "Please, please, please can we stay?"

Uh-oh.

I laugh to break the awkwardness. "Ha. Bevin, your little-kid imitation is really good." She looks confused for a second and then catches on.

"I've been working on it," she says. And then AGE laugh too, and I feel reassured that my work with Bevin is actually paying off.

I quickly text my mom that we're going to grab dinner on the boardwalk and that we'll be back at the pharmacy before closing.

People start coming and lining up outside of Hotdogger & Co. I doubt they're all participating; I think they just like to watch people stuff their faces.

We have a really good spot toward the front since we've basically been here all day.

We're watching the staff set up the tables and the big bins of hot dogs when I feel a tap on my shoulder.

"Lucy?"

I turn around. My heart is pounding because I obviously know that voice. I'd know it anywhere, even in a loud, screaming concert with a million people.

"Hi, Sun." I try to act calm even though I'm a total idiot—Sunny told me about this event weeks ago. I completely forgot she was coming, and I never texted her back.

But she's always busy with Evan. I doubt she even cares that I'm here.

"Who are you here with? I stopped by the pharmacy and then texted, to see if you wanted to come, and I got no response," she says, sounding befuddled.

"Oh, just Bevin and AGE." I point at them. They're watching us talk, and it's a little freaky.

I'm sure Sunny's confused since I don't usually hang out with them, but I can't explain with them listening in.

"Oh." She raises her eyebrows and stays silent for a few seconds. "Well, come on, let's go up front."

I turn around and look at Bevin and AGE, and then back at Sunny. Now I'm the confused one.

I laugh. "Sun, you're participating? We were planning on staying here and watching famous hot-dog eaters, like that guy who always does the Coney Island contest."

Sunny cracks up. "No. You and Yamir are participating!

145

Remember? We signed you guys up at my house that day after the Earth Club Earth Day party."

I try to think back, but I can barely remember anything from before we got the grant and started the construction, from before Sunny and Evan started going out, and before Claudia came home and Bevin moved to Connecticut. Everything happened so fast that it's all a blur.

"I think I'm going to beat my record," Yamir says, seemingly coming out of nowhere. "Last year I had eleven. I can totally do it."

Is this really happening?

"Last chance to sign up," a woman yells out to the crowd. "We had a few cancellations, so we have a few more spots!"

"Sunny, you can do it too." I pat her on the back, trying to inch her forward to sign up.

"Are you kidding?" She looks at me like I just told her to swim across the Atlantic Ocean. "I'm not doing it."

"You're not gonna bail, right Luce-Juice?" Yamir grabs my hands, and then raises them in the air like we're at some kind of political rally or something. "Luce-Juice! Luce-Juice!"

I let go of his hands. "I guess not," I say quietly.

"You're in the contest?" Annabelle squeaks. "Is that why you've been hanging out here all day?"

"No, I forgot Sunny signed me up." I laugh, then look over at Bevin. She shouldn't enter this contest. She spits when she eats and gets food all over her face, and a hot-dog-eating contest isn't a good thing for her personality make-over.

To be honest, I'm a little embarrassed that I'm doing it.

Bevin goes to the bathroom with AGE and I'm left standing by myself for a minute, wondering if entering a hot-dog-eating contest is a huge game changer with Yamir. Maybe, if I do it, he won't see me in a girly way anymore. I'll just be some competitor, like one of the guys, and then we'll never go on a real date.

I tap him on the shoulder. "Yamir, I think I changed my mind. My stomach is kind of weird all of a sudden and—"

"Oh, come on!" he says. "You'll be great."

I tell myself that it's fine, that we're doing something together, that he wants me to be a part of it. So what that I forgot about it until now? Maybe it's better that I forgot, that way I wasn't nervous all day. I guess I was so busy thinking about Bevin that I wasn't thinking about myself.

The people who work at Hotdogger & Co. seat each of us at a little table with a plate overflowing with hot dogs. It's a no-buns kind of event and we can have as much water as we want.

"Don't fill up on water," Yamir whispers to me. "Just eat. Don't think."

The woman wearing a giant hot dog costume reads out the rules. There are fifteen people participating and what seems like a hundred spectators. Of our friends, Yamir and I are the only ones participating. Sunny, Evan, Clint, and Anthony are standing around us cheering, and so are Bevin and AGE.

"Go, Lucy! Go, Yamir! Go, Lucy and Yamir!" They keep saying it over and over again. It's a nice feeling when someone cheers for you.

The hot dog costume lady blows her whistle, and we all start eating.

It's weird to shove hot dogs in your mouth while people cheer for you, but then every few seconds, I look over at Yamir sitting next to me and he smiles this crooked smile because his mouth is full of hot dogs and it makes me laugh. And then I just keep eating. And for the first time in a while, I'm not thinking about the spa and Anais and all of that, I'm just thinking about eating hot dogs, and sitting next to Yamir, and Sunny and everyone cheering for us.

So I just keep eating and smiling and then before I know it, the hot dog lady is grabbing my arm and waving it in the air. "We have a wiener!" she yells. "Fifteen hot dogs!"

I can't believe I ate fifteen hot dogs. For the last few, I was just focusing on my plate and eating and thinking about Yamir and me. If we got married one day, we could tell everyone about this day and all the crazy things we did together.

I look down the row at my competition. It appears they all stopped eating a few seconds ago. I hadn't even noticed. Even Yamir is just sitting there, holding his stomach.

"What's your name?" hot dog lady whispers.

"Lucy." After I say it, my stomach starts to get funny and I wonder if drinking water will make it feel better or worse.

"Lucy here has just won unlimited hot dogs for an entire year!" the hot dog lady yells and hands me a giant check, but it doesn't really make sense, since there's no dollar amount on it. It just says UNLIMITED HOT DOGS FOR A YEAR. It doesn't even say dates or anything, but I guess they know when they're giving it to me.

"Yay, Lucy!" Sunny yells, and everyone starts cheering and it's all I can do not to throw up. Sunny squeezes her way to the front of the crowd so she can talk to me without anyone hearing. "When you've recovered, we have to talk."

"About?"

"About why you ditched me for AGE . . . and Bevin."

"Sunny, come on," I start, but then she gets a call from her mom and they need to figure out where they're meeting her, so she walks away to talk to her.

"You rocked that, Luce-Juice," Yamir says. "I'd kiss you right now, but we both ate a million hot dogs, so it would be kind of gross."

At first I don't process what he just said because I'm so focused on my insane thirst, and the fact that Sunny's really mad at me, and the fact that I just ate fifteen hot dogs. My mouth is too tired to say anything out loud.

Yamir just said he would kiss me. I wonder if he was serious.

"Lucy!" I hear Bevin yelling from the bench a few feet away from us. "Georgina's mom can drive us to the pharmacy! She'll be here in five minutes—come on."

I yell back OK, and then when I turn to say good-bye to Yamir and find Sunny, I see them already walking away, toward the parking lot.

Bevin arranged a ride home for us, with Georgina Emminson of all people, probably the most popular girl in our grade. Yamir said he'd kiss me, but we'd just eaten a million hot dogs. Sunny thinks I ditched her.

All of these things are bizarre, and I want to figure them out. But I don't know where to start.

I think about Bevin and I wonder if it's just all about leaving your comfort zone. I threw her in with strangers and she did fine. But when she hung around me and the spa, she was the most annoying girl in the world. Maybe people just need to shake things up every once in a while.

Maybe that's what it would be like if Dad came back to Connecticut for real. It would just shake things up. And maybe that would be good. Or maybe it would be bad. It's hard to say for sure, and in the meantime, it's a lot to worry about.

Lucy's tip for becoming a better person:
Never tell someone they look tired.
They don't want to hear it.

Anais needs to leave town for a few days to handle all the filing for the spa inspections and certifications. Mom, Grandma, Anais, and Gary have been working on the paperwork for weeks now, and it always seems like they're tearing their hair out over it.

Morrie had to come in and sign some papers since he's the accountant and financial adviser. They've had to get forms notarized and go back and forth to the bank and city hall three million times.

It all seems really annoying and frustrating. Like if they forget to cross one *t*, it'll all fall apart. I hope not, but it seems that way.

So before Anais leaves she wants us all to have a meeting so we can catch each other up on what we've been doing. Unfortunately she's leaving by ten, so our meeting is happening at eight A.M.

We're all sitting in the Relaxation Room since none of the other meeting areas are big enough to hold all of us. But the Relaxation Room is the most calming, so it's obviously the best spot for an early-morning meeting.

"This is gonna be fast, right?" Bevin whispers in my ear.

I shrug. I don't even know why she's sitting here. She doesn't have to be. "I don't know. Why?"

"I told Annabelle we'd meet her at the pool in her neighborhood." She pauses. "You know where that is, right?"

"You made plans with Annabelle without me?" I ask. I can't tell if I'm annoyed or hurt or impressed. Hanging out with AGE was just supposed to be practice for Bevin. I don't really want to make a habit of it. They're super-popular, and they're not always the nicest girls.

"Well, I—"

"OK, thanks for meeting me so early," Anais interrupts. Claudia flicks Bean's shoulder because he's falling asleep on the couch with his head back and his mouth wide open. He jerks forward. "I'll be gone for a few days and I just want to make sure we're all on the same page."

Each week that Anais has been here, she's gotten progressively stricter and more stressed. Maybe it's harder work than she thought it was going to be, or maybe we're just hard to work with. Either way, her job is starting to seem like less fun than it was at first.

"Our website and e-mail addresses are all set up." She looks over at my mom. "Thank you to Jane for finding that wonderful web designer and for working with him on the layout. I've worked with him on all the technical stuff, and he's great."

"Oh, my pleasure. Seth's an old friend from college. He does great work. And would you believe his first career was veterinary work. Unbelievable." Grandma pats her leg and whispers something in her ear and then Mom stops talking.

"So the URL is pinkandgreenspa.com and it will be linked from the Old Mill Pharmacy site. I've made a few e-mail addresses and there's room to make more. So far we have info@ pinkandgreenspa.com, appointments@pinkandgreenspa.com, and press@pinkandgreenspa.com. We need to make sure we're checking these at least once an hour in the coming weeks, so I've made it easy. The password for every e-mail is Desberg384. We can change it later, but that way it's easy and we know it so we can all check it and make sure everything is covered."

I'm so glad she just told everyone the password, because if she had done it in private and I was left out, I would have been so upset.

"We're still waiting on the shipment of brochures, business cards, and other marketing materials." Anais looks over at me. "Thanks to Lucy's friends and their family, we've secured a great price on printing."

I smile. It feels good to be thanked, even if it's just for knowing Sunny and the Ramals.

"We're still a little short-staffed, but Claudia and Bean will be continuing the interviews and demo procedures this week while I'm away." She looks down at her notebook. "Jane has to finish the last few supply orders. And then when I'm back, Doris and I need to finalize all the plans for the grand opening, if we want a booth on the street or how we want to approach it."

"A booth on the street could be great!" I exclaim. "We could have one of those portable massage chairs out there, and give free two-minute massages to bring people in."

Everyone's nodding. "That's an idea," Mom says.

"We could also sell some skin-care products in the booth," Claudia adds, "and take appointments."

Mom's phone starts ringing and she hops up from the couch. "I gotta take this, guys. It's Sam calling from London. Be right back."

Grandma puts her head back and closes her eyes for a second, like she's about to scream but trying to hold it in. I wonder why. Maybe she's mad at my dad for something, but I can't imagine what. She always seemed to like my dad, even now that they never see each other.

Mom closes the pharmacy office door to have the phone conversation with my dad. I would pay a million dollars—if I had a million dollars—to find out what that phone call is all about.

"OK, so I think we're set. Good work on everything, guys." Anais smiles. "We have a few weeks until the grand opening and I think we're in good shape. Cross your fingers that everything works out with the inspections."

I stand up and make an over-the-top crossing fingers gesture, but no one seems to find it funny. "I'll let you know when I get the final numbers on appointments from Sarabeth," I add, just so they take me seriously. "She said eight bridesmaids, but I want to make sure I know what each person is getting done."

"Thanks, Lucy." Anais gets up and straightens her flouncy skirt. "See you all in a few days."

Bevin and I are the first ones out of the meeting (except for my mom, who left early to take the call).

"I'm going to run an errand with my dad, and then he'll drop me off at Annabelle's pool. She texted me the address. Meet me there," Bevin says, more like a statement than a question.

"Um, OK." All I can think about right now is checking all the new e-mail addresses! It may be really pathetic, but it feels so official to have our own business e-mail accounts.

"I mean, you're not too busy for some swimming, right?" she continues.

I look at her, confused. She's asking me to go, but maybe that's just because she's being nice. Maybe this is the next step in her makeover, and she should go on her own. After all, it's not like Annabelle texted me about the plans—she texted Bevin.

"OK, have fun," I say, smiling. I decide to leave it open, and see if she presses the issue.

"OK." She makes a puckered kissy face. "Smooches."

So we still need to work on that obnoxious kissy face of hers.

Bevin heads out with Gary, and since my mom is in the pharmacy office, I sprint over to the spa reception area and sit down in the comfy rolling chair. I turn on the MacBook and follow the links to the Pink & Green e-mail.

I feel like I could stay in this seat forever. I'd love watching all the customers come in and out. I could always play online if I got bored. The computer is sparkly and shiny and superfast.

Unfortunately there isn't much e-mail to check. Just a

few registration sign-up things for Boat Fest, and some tips to enhance your e-mail and get the most out of your online experience.

Oh well. I'll keep checking, at least once an hour like Anais said.

While I'm at the computer, I check my personal e-mail, where there's a reminder that the southeastern Connecticut and Rhode Island small business owners' meeting is happening tonight! How did I not realize that? It's taking place at the Bayberry Cove Library, which is about four towns away from Old Mill. That's where Sunny's aunt and uncle and her cousin Asha live.

OK, Lucy, think. I need to figure out what I'm going to tell Mom and Grandma and Claudia, some reason why I need to go all the way to the Bayberry Cove Library. And now I don't even have to worry that Anais will be at the meeting because I know for sure she's out of town! The timing couldn't be more perfect.

My mom pops her head into the spa area. "So sorry to run out like this, Luce, but I have another meeting at the *Old Mill Observer*." She winks at me. "Top secret, but I think they're going to let me write some articles. Not really a staff writer, I won't have an office, but they're pleased with my writing."

"Mom!" I shout, and she shushes me. "That is so amazing! It's your dream!"

"I know," she whispers. "But let's keep it quiet. Nothing's certain yet, OK?

"I should be back later tonight. I have this meeting and then I'm going with one of the editors to this journalism and business conference," she tells me. "There's grilled chicken salad in the fridge for you." She leans over and kisses me on the cheek. "Make sure you're checking the e-mails while I'm gone."

I nod. This sneaking out to the meeting thing is going to be easier than I thought. It doesn't even seem like anyone's around. Claudia and Bean may be here, but they don't pay attention to me anyway.

And then I hear Grandma whistling.

OK, one tiny obstacle left.

"Lucy," she calls. "Come help me, please, doll."

I run over and find Grandma hovering over a box of washcloths. "Luce, Eli's in the spa area, helping to install that closet-organizer system. When he's done, I want you to arrange all these towels by size. Can you handle that?"

I nod. "Duh. Of course I can."

"Thanks, love." She gives me a hug.

"Oh, but, Grams, I need to go to the library tonight for

Earth Club research," I tell her. I wasn't even really planning what I was going to say; the lie is just coming out, flowing normally. "So I'll be leaving at six, OK?"

"What about dinner?" Grandma asks. "I don't want you skipping meals like your sister. You're still growing and you need to eat."

"Oh, don't worry, I'm going out for dinner with Sunny after," I tell her. Another lie.

"Well, let Claudia or me know if you need a ride, and please take this box over to the spa area. Eli should be done soon." Grandma ties her hair back in this pretty floral hair band. "Mr. Tuscano, I'm on my way to give you that prescription!" She jogs over to the prescription counter. I'm glad to have a grandma that can still jog, even if it only is a few feet.

I carry that box of washcloths over and Eli is still finishing organizing the closet. Claudia and Bean are conducting another interview and I don't want to disturb them. I step outside the building for a second and quickly call Sunny.

"Did you throw up?" she asks me before saying hello.

At first I'm confused and then I remember the hot-dog-eating contest. Wow, that seems like forever ago already. "No, not at all. I was fine!" I laugh. "Hope that's not even grosser."

"Well, you certainly impressed the boys," she says. "Yamir was telling my dad about it this morning. He was like 'isn't that so awesome?' and 'she's so cool' and then when I caught him and he noticed me, he started blushing. It was funny."

Yamir was bragging about me to his dad? Sure, it was only about eating hot dogs, but that's still pretty cool.

"I need to ask you a favor," I tell her. "Please say yes. If you're thinking about saying no, just remember all I did for you by joining Earth Club and helping you with Evan and all of that." I pause. "OK?"

"First of all we have to discuss you and Bevin becoming BFFs with AGE," she starts.

"We aren't BFF," I say. "They're basically just people for Bevin to hang out with so she can learn to be social. But I need you to say you'll help me."

"Lucy! First of all, what a weird reason to hang out with people. Second of all, I can't say yes if I don't know what it is. What if you're asking me to jump into the river from a high bridge or something?"

I groan. "It's nothing like that. I just need you to come with me to Bayberry Cove Library tonight. You can sit and read in the YA section while we're there, I just need you to come with me so it doesn't look strange."

"Huh? Explain."

So I tell her all about the small business owners' group and how I feel it's important for me to go. "I want to get advice on how to be taken more seriously in the business," I add. "And they have meetings once a month, I think, and this one isn't too far away."

"But my aunt and uncle and Asha and Raj live in Bayberry Cove," she tells me. "So what if they see us?"

"Do they normally hang out at the library?" I laugh.

"No, they all have iPads and download like forty e-books a day, but that's a whole 'nother story." She sniffles; she always has summer allergies. "Fine, I'll go. But what should we say our reason for going is?"

I peek into the spa window to make sure Eli's still working on the closet. I don't want to shirk any responsibilities here. I need to make sure I unpack that box before I leave. "We'll say they have books and stuff we need for Earth Club that Old Mill and Waterside libraries don't have."

Sunny sniffles again. "OK, sure. It's twenty-five minutes away, though. My mom will probably just wait while we go in."

Darn. That won't work. "Here's an idea. I'll make Claudia and Bean drive us, and your mom can pick us up. We'll tell her a later time so she doesn't see the meeting in progress."

"Oh! I have an amazing idea. There's that famous lobster roll place a few blocks away," Sunny says. "Asha's taken me there a million times. We'll call when the meeting's over and tell my mom to meet us there and we'll get lobster rolls after the meeting!"

"Genius, Sunny!" I shout. "You always solve problems with food. I love it!"

She cracks up. "OK, I'm not gonna invite Yamir or Evan because then there's more of a chance of them spilling the beans. What time are we going?"

"Be ready at six. The meeting starts at seven."

"Got it," she says, then pauses. "You know we're making up this whole elaborate lie just so you can go to a business owners' meeting? That's really, really lame."

"Gee, thanks." She was being so nice up until now.

"I'm just saying. Usually teenagers make up this stuff to sneak out to concerts or to meet famous people or go to parties or something." She laughs. "But a discussion group? It's funny."

"Fine. It's funny." I'm not laughing.

"Don't take yourself so seriously, Luce." Sunny pauses and waits for me to say something. "Fine, whatever. See you at six."

Go for night walks and count the stars.

I still don't understand why you need to go all the way to Bayberry Cove to do research, Lucy," Claudia says as I'm rushing her to leave. "We have computers, the Internet, databases, whatever, you don't need to go to a library so far away."

"They have a whole environmental Going Green section," I tell her.

"They do?" Bean asks. "That's pretty impressive."

"Let's just go. Come on. We're going to be late to pick up Sunny." I drop the subject because all I need is Bean coming in with me to peruse the section. Maybe I'm not as good a liar as I thought I was.

Claudia groans. "We've been busy here all day. We're not on call to be your chauffeur."

"Well, Grandma's busy, and Mom's busy," I say. "Besides,

you can go to Lobster Landing after you drop me off. Best lobster rolls in all of Connecticut, ten years in a row."

"Oh, yeah!" Claudia exclaims. "Bean, get ready. You've never had a lobster roll like the ones at Lobster Landing. It's right on the water and it's so nice."

"Bonus!" Bean high-fives me. "We get to chauffeur Lucy and Sunny and get lobster rolls. This is the best day of the summer so far."

I roll my eyes but eventually start laughing. Bean's not a bad guy. He's a little doofy, but he's funny sometimes, and he loves my sister, so I guess he can't be that awful.

We're in the car on the way to Sunny's house and I get a sinking-stomach feeling, similar to how I felt after I ate all the hot dogs. What if this is a huge mistake? I could be turned away from the meeting, or maybe someone there knows Mom or Grandma or even Anais. I should have thought this through. I need a wig or a hat or crazy glasses.

I need a full disguise.

"I'll be right back." I hop out of the car and go into Sunny's house. I don't wait for Claudia or Bean to ask me why I'm going in; I just go.

"Hello, Lucy darling," Mrs. Ramal says.

"Hi. Um, can I run upstairs? I need to get something from Sunny."

She nods, confused.

"Sunny!" I burst into her room. "I need a disguise. What if someone recognizes me?" I don't wait for a response. I just start rifling through her closet, looking at her hats and sweaters and anything I can find. "Do you have a wig?"

"Lucy." She puts her hand on my shoulder. "Calm down." She hands me her old glasses that had a very light prescription. "Wear these."

I put them on and I'm surprised at how cute I look in the wire frames.

"Even if I give you a hat, will you really wear it indoors?"

I shrug. "I don't know. I just think I should look a little different, a little unlike myself."

Sunny looks at her watch. "We need to go or you're going to be late." She's still looking through her closet. "I know! A sari!"

"Huh?"

"You're kind of tan now, so you can just look like a pale Indian girl." She finds the prettiest sari in her closet and hands it to me. It's pale pink and turquoise with little silver beading. It could probably pass as some kind of artsy sundress. "Go change."

I listen to her and when I come out of the bathroom, Sunny tells me how pretty I look.

"But won't your family wonder why I'm wearing this?" I ask.

She hesitates for a second. "Give me your clothes."

She runs back into the bathroom and puts on my jean cutoff shorts and my ribbed yellow tank top.

"We traded clothes! Perfect explanation!"

I don't have the heart to tell her it doesn't make sense really since she wasn't wearing the sari before. Sunny's trying so hard and not being mean; I can't ruin that. And we run out of the house so fast, no one really sees us. We just yell good-bye as we're out the door.

On the way over, I'm really, really nervous. I keep wanting to ask Sunny questions—like should I say my name is Sunny Ramal? Should I make up a new name? I thought I had this all planned out but now I'm not so sure. I worry that if I say my name is Lucy Desberg, someone will recognize it and figure me out.

"Why are you wearing that to go do research for Earth Club?" Claudia asks me after a few minutes. I wonder what took her so long. I guess she's been distracted by the book she's reading.

"I love wearing Sunny's clothes," I tell her, "and I rarely get to anymore."

"Oh-kay." Claudia drags out the word.

Bean is actually a very slow, cautious driver, or maybe it's just because he's driving Grandma's car and wants to be careful. Whatever it is, it feels like it's taking a billion years to get to the Bayberry Cove Library. And the longer it takes, the more nervous I get and the more I regret deciding to do this.

Sunny squeezes my hand. "You are acting so weird," she whispers.

After what feels like a two-hour drive, we finally get to the Bayberry Cove Library.

"So Sunny's mom is picking you up?" Claudia turns around from the front seat.

"Yup."

"If the line's really long at Lobster Landing, we can always come to the library after and wait for you to be done," she adds.

"No, no, that's OK," I say really fast.

Claudia crinkles her eyes at me. "You're odd, Lucy. But I love you anyway."

Sunny and I get out of the car and walk toward the double doors of the library. We watch Bean and Claudia drive away.

"Are you ready?" Sunny asks me.

"I don't know why I'm so nervous."

She shrugs. "You'll be fine." I clutch her arm, suddenly

feeling wobbly, and she widens her eyes at me and breathes through her nose. "Can you stop acting like this? You're driving me crazy."

"Sunny, you agreed to come. I need your help."

She ignores me.

"Should I make up a new name? Where should I say my spa is? I'm so scared. I don't want this to end up getting back to my mom or grandma or Anais. Then I'll really be in trouble." I sit down on the sidewalk outside of the library for a second. I need to think.

"Say your name is Lucy Ramal. Your spa is in New York City but you're back and forth to your summer home in Waterside, so you wanted to get some advice." Sunny blurts out this list as fast as she can. "No one will find you out."

"Maybe I should be Louise Ramal?"

"Fine." Sunny pats me on the back, but it's an impatient pat, not a nice one. "Now go. You're going to be late."

Lucy's tip for becoming a better person:
Always say "Thank you" when
someone holds a door for you.

May I help you?" a woman at the reference desk asks me as I walk in. I guess I look lost. Sunny was planning to wait outside for a second or two and then come in so it didn't look suspicious.

"Oh, I'm here for the small business owners' group," I tell her, trying to sound as adult as possible.

"Sure, they're in the children's corner, in the back on the left-hand side." She smiles. "Beautiful sari, by the way."

"Thanks." I wonder if she thinks I'm Indian. I kind of hope so.

As I'm walking over, I feel my phone vibrating. I take it out because I think that it's Sunny, but when I look at it, it's Bevin calling.

I debate answering versus letting it go to voice mail but in the end, I decide to answer it.

"Lucy, I need your help," Bevin says as soon as I say hello.

"Can I call you back?" I whisper. "I'm at the library."

"What?" she yells.

"Never mind. Can I please call you back later?"

"I really need to talk to you," she says.

Out of the corner of my eye, I see the small business owners' group gathering. The meeting is going to start any minute. But Bevin needs me. I don't know what to do.

"I'm so sorry, Bevin, but I can't use cell phones in here. I promise to call back soon. Bye."

I hang up before she can say anything else. I feel bad, but I really don't have a choice. There's a huge sign with a cell phone in a red circle with a line through it.

I want to put Bevin's call and Sunny's weirdness out of my head, so I can focus on the task at hand: this meeting.

It's funny that this group is meeting in the children's section, but it makes sense since most little kids are home by now. The people sit in regular-sized chairs, with all of the little chairs stacked up in a corner.

"Hello, my name is Louise Ramal. I'm here for the meeting," I say to the lady standing up. Everyone else is sitting down. They all stare at me. I'm pretty sure one man is about to tell me to leave— he's got a scowl on his face like I've just interrupted his important conversation. I square my shoulders and try to look like Anais.

"Welcome. We'll be starting in just a minute." The lady smiles. At least she's nice. I let out a breath I didn't know I'd been holding. "Please fill out this contact information sheet. That way we'll be able to keep in touch, alert you to the next meetings, etc."

"OK."

I sit down on one of the chairs on the edge of the circle where there aren't any other people. I need space to fill out this form because I'm really not sure what to write. Out of the corner of my eye, I see Sunny coming in and talking to the same person at the reference desk. Then I see her walking over to the young adult section, which is very close to where our meeting is taking place. I hope she doesn't make faces at me and make me laugh. She looks grumpy, so I doubt she will.

This form is tricky because it asks for addresses of the business, phone numbers, and all that stuff. I decide to just write down my cell number and my e-mail and say that we're in the very beginning stages of opening our spa so I don't have contact info there yet.

That seems believable, I think.

Soon the lady collects the sheets and calls the meeting to order. There are about fifteen people here and they all look like my mom—natural, relaxed, attentive.

"Welcome to the third meeting of the southeastern Connecticut and Rhode Island small business owners' discussion group," the lady starts. "For those newcomers, my name is Ruthie, and my husband and I just sold the Utopia Body and Wellness Spa in Providence, Rhode Island. We're in the process of figuring out our next steps." She owned a spa! It's such a great coincidence I almost can't believe it. She could really help us out. She smiles and she's so calming that all of my nervousness just washes away. Even if I do get discovered and found out for being a liar, I doubt she would get mad at me. She's too chill. "Let's go around the circle and say our name and what type of business we're opening."

The lady next to me starts and then goes around the circle the other way, which means I'll be the last one to say my name.

Most of them are from Rhode Island, which puts me more at ease. There's less of a chance that they'll recognize me or know my mom or grandma.

"I'm Louise Ramal, and my family and I are in the beginning stages of opening a spa in Manhattan. We're back and forth to our summer home in Waterside, and I stumbled upon this meeting and figured I'd check it out." I giggle out of nervousness and hope that I didn't just ramble on for way too long. Everyone else's introductions were just four seconds each.

"Welcome, Louise," the moderator says. "It's good you're

here in the beginning stages since there's so much that goes into opening any type of business."

A lady across the circle from me raises her hand. "Louise, honey, are you here with a parent or something?" she asks, smiling but confused.

"Oh, right, I'm a kid." I laugh. "You probably noticed that. Well, um, my parents were here with me, and my grandfather was staying home with my younger brother, but then my brother got sick, so they went home, and I just decided to stay." I laugh again. I need to stop this nervous laugh. "So I'll just sit and listen. If that's, um, OK."

Ruthie nods. "Sure. We're happy to have you, Louise."

As I suspected, much of what is discussed is way over my head. Stuff about plumbing and construction and zoning and permits. They also talk about how to fire a frustrating employee and how to properly budget for the slow periods. I stay quiet most of the time, but jot down notes every few minutes. Some of what they're saying could be very helpful later on.

With about ten minutes left in the meeting, the only man here raises his hand. "I know we touched on this a little bit," he starts, and I try hard to remember his name and where he's from, but I'm drawing a blank. "I'm opening my second restaurant in a few months, same name and brand and everything, but I'm tripped up again on the inspection stuff. It seems Connecticut is much harder for inspections than Rhode Island, and I feel like all the paperwork is getting lost in the shuffle."

A few ladies give him answers that sound really complicated to me. They involve calling someone in Hartford and then making sure all of their yellow forms are filled out in triplicate, not to worry about the green forms, and then keeping copies of everything in a safety-deposit box.

At this point in the meeting it's hard for me to sit still. I can see Sunny in the section next to us looking at her watch every few seconds and groaning, and all I can think about are lobster rolls and root beers. And of course calling Bevin back. I can't even imagine what happened to her. She could have gone back to her old self by now; she could be saying embarrassing things about me to everyone in Old Mill. The longer I wait, the worse it can get.

I'm glad I came. But now I need the meeting to end.

A few minutes later, Ruthie thanks everyone for coming and people start to leave.

"Louise," Ruthie calls to me. "I just wanted to let you know that if your parents have any questions about the group, they can e-mail me."

"Oh, OK, thanks."

"And I hope your brother feels better." She smiles.

Is she onto me? I can't tell.

"Oh, thanks. You know kids, they always get fevers."

"Right."

I pretend to peruse the children's section for a few minutes and then I quietly walk over to Sunny.

"Can we go now?" she says immediately.

"How did I sound?" I ask. I kind of expect her to say something mean, since I made her wait and she's been in such a bad mood.

"Great."

"You were really listening?" I ask her. "You promise?"

"Totally." She smiles, and I'm so relieved. "So—lobster rolls?"

"You know it." We leave the library and walk the few blocks to Lobster Landing. We can smell the delicious salty sea air as we walk, and I just want to grab a blanket and lie down on the beach and stare out at the ocean and up at the sky and not think about anything else.

There's a line at Lobster Landing, of course. It's always packed, any time of the day.

"You owe me for tonight," Sunny says after we've been quiet for a few minutes.

"Huh?"

"Evan asked me to go to the beach with him. Doesn't that sound so romantic? But I had to tell him no so I could come with you." She glares at me.

I stay quiet for a few seconds. I'm not sure what she wants me to say. "Oh, well, thanks."

"That's it? Just thanks?"

"I don't know, Sunny. You didn't give me a kidney or anything." I roll my eyes. "Sorry you gave up a night with your boyfriend."

I wish this conversation had never started, because I'm getting a nervous feeling in my stomach, and it's going to ruin my whole lobster roll experience.

"You don't get it," Sunny says after another few minutes of silence. "You don't have a real boyfriend, so you don't get it."

When did Sunny get so mean?

"I'm not talking to you now," I tell her. "I just want to eat my lobster roll in peace. Tell your mom to come pick us up."

"And you only call me when you need me to help you. Hanging out with AGE? Not telling me? Spending so much time with Bevin?" She sniffles. "I don't get you anymore."

I don't say anything because we're at the front of the line. I order a Connecticut-style lobster roll, chips, a pickle, and a root beer. Sunny orders a Maine-style and a cream soda.

We sit at one of the white picnic tables right on the water.

Lights twinkle all around us and boats sway back and forth where they're docked. It would be a perfect Connecticut night except for the feeling like I have a knotted rope in my stomach.

"You don't have anything to say to the fact that you've basically been avoiding me all summer?" Sunny asks.

I put down my lobster roll and say, "Sunny, how can you say that? You've been with Evan all summer. You don't even want to hang out with me."

"You know that's not true." She leans forward onto the table and glares at me. "You make no effort. You wait for me to call you. And when I don't, you hang out with AGE."

"That was once. Sheesh."

"You know I'm right and you can't even admit it or say you're sorry," Sunny says. "Let's just not talk for a bit."

We eat our lobster rolls in silence and we might as well be eating lima beans—that's how depressing this feels.

I debate it over and over again in my head and then I realize I can't just let this go.

"Sunny, how can you say that I need to apologize when it was really mean of you to say that I owe you for tonight because you could have been with your boyfriend," I tell her. "Yes, you have a boyfriend, but you also have a best friend."

She looks at me and I can tell she's not sorry. "You sound like some kind of cheesy inspirational quote people put on

Facebook. And besides, you haven't been acting like a best friend."

I look down at my plate. I still have half a lobster roll and my chips, but I can't even eat them. And I can't just stay quiet either. "But, Sunny, saying I owe you and that you gave something up takes all the niceness out of what you did."

She rolls her eyes. "The world doesn't revolve around you, Lucy."

"I know," I mumble.

"I like helping you, but you can't expect that I'm always going to do it." Her phone vibrates on the table and she looks at it. "My mom will be here in five minutes. Finish eating, OK?"

"I'm not hungry."

"Lucy, come on. Stop being so sensitive."

"I'm not sensitive. You're mean."

"Fine. I'm mean." She stands up to throw away her garbage. "Then if I'm mean, I might as well tell you that Yamir doesn't really like you. He never really liked you. I overheard him on the phone with Clint the other day and he was talking about how that girl Arianna in his grade is really pretty."

I stand up to throw away my garbage and when I get back to the table, Sunny's already walking away, toward the street and her mom's car.

I can't believe she just said that.

I don't know how this night changed tone so fast. She was supportive about me wearing her sari, but after that she was totally different, like she flicked a switch.

Maybe it was out of line to ask her to hang out at the library while I had the meeting. Maybe I asked too much of her. But even so, she's my best friend, and that's what best friends do for each other. Right?

Lucy's tip for a great summer:
Spend a lot of time on a lounge chair.

Sunny's mom notices something is up because she says "You two are very quiet" at least three times, but unlike my mom, she doesn't press it. She senses that we just want to be quiet and she lets it go.

We pull into my driveway and I realize that I'm going to have to say some kind of good-bye, and whatever I say is going to seem awkward.

I unbuckle my seat belt and say, "Thank you Mrs. Ramal. Bye, Sunny," and leave it at that.

I go over the day and night in my head and I can't figure out what set Sunny off. She's really that mad about me hanging out with AGE? She knows we don't even really like them. She knows I was just doing it to help Bevin. Doesn't she? And then I wonder if what she said about Yamir is true. I want to just come out and ask him, but I don't think I can.

I walk inside and my mom, grandma, and Claudia are all sitting in the living room.

This can't be good.

"Luce, come sit with us," Grandma says.

"Be right there," I yell back. I run upstairs and drop my bag and splash some cold water on my face. All I want to do right now is throw on my bathing suit and go for a night swim. We have lights out there, so it's safe, and I can just float around on my pink raft and process everything that has happened without anyone bothering me. I throw Sunny's sari in the corner of my room. I decide to put on my bathing suit now and grab a towel so I can go out and swim as soon as we're done talking. Then I can call Bevin back while relaxing on a lounge chair.

"What's up?" I say as soon as I'm sitting down on one of the living room armchairs. "Oh, Mom, how'd your *Old Mill Observer* meeting go?"

"It went well, Luce. Thanks." She smiles, but I can tell there's something hanging in the air here. I'm not exactly sure what it is.

I keep waiting for someone to say something. Then I try to convince myself that this weird feeling is all in my head. Maybe they're just sitting and relaxing and enjoying each other's company.

"Lucy, I just got off the phone with Gary," Grandma says.

"Apparently Bevin got stuck at Annabelle Wilson's house, and she hoped you were going to meet her, but you didn't, and Bevin got upset. I don't really know the whole story."

"What? No. Bevin's friends with them now. She was fine on her own. She said so herself."

"Why is Bevin friends with Annabelle Wilson?" Claudia asks. "Why doesn't she just hang out with you and Sunny?"

Claudia's the kind of older sister who really knows her little sister's friends. It's usually nice. But at a time like this, it would be easier if she didn't have a clue.

"We met them at the boardwalk one day and they hit it off. I was trying to help Bevin, you know, become a little bit more social, and like, you know, help her be a little more normal." I feel my cheeks getting hot. I don't even know what I'm saying anymore.

"I don't understand what's really going on here," Mom says. "Why is Bevin upset?"

"I have no idea, honestly," I tell them. "I'll call her. OK?"

"That's a good idea," Grandma says, sitting up straighter on the couch.

I can't believe this is happening. First Sunny yells at me and then tells me Yamir doesn't like me anymore, and now I'm in trouble for trying to help Bevin become a better version of herself.

"I'm going swimming," I tell them, and leave the living room. No one tries to stop me.

I hear mumbles and whispers as I'm walking out the back door to the deck, but I ignore them.

This has to be some kind of joke. Some kind of bad dream.

I throw my towel down on the lounge chair and cannonball off the diving board. I feel myself sinking down to the bottom of the pool and then I pop back up and jump onto my favorite pink raft.

I float and float and float and I keep telling myself to think because if I think hard enough, I can figure out what to tell Sunny and Bevin and my family. But nothing comes to me. I guess it's because I don't think any of what happened is my fault. But if I tell them that, it will sound defensive, like I'm blaming other people for my problems.

The worst part of it is, even with all of the drama with Sunny and the weirdness with this Bevin situation, I'm still thinking about what Sunny said about Yamir, and how he thought that girl Arianna was pretty.

I need to know if that's true. Because if Yamir doesn't like me anymore, then I can stop worrying about it. I definitely don't need something else to worry about, so it might be a relief.

I spend the next hour or so floating and then my mom

pops her head out. "Luce, it's almost eleven thirty. Come in, please. I don't like you out here while everyone else is asleep."

I get out of the pool, shower, and get into pajamas. I write three different e-mails to Yamir but I don't send any of them. I write out text message after text message but then click DIS-CARD after each one.

I don't know what to say, so I decide to just leave it as is for tonight. I'm too tired to deal with anything else.

I check my e-mail one more time before bed, thinking that maybe Sunny e-mailed me an apology or something, but I only have one e-mail in my in-box. It's from Ruthie, the woman from the small business meeting.

Hello Louise,

I just wanted to tell you it was a pleasure to meet you at tonight's gathering. I noticed you were very quiet, so please feel free to e-mail me any questions or con-cerns you may have. Our next meeting won't be until September since so many of us will be away in August.

Best wishes,

Ruthie

Well, that was nice. At least a grown-up stranger who thinks my name is Louise cares about my questions or concerns.

I've been putting it off all night, but after hours of tossing and turning, I decide that there's one thing I have to do.

I started Bevin on this path and I can't just abandon her now. She stays up late, so I know it's OK to text her.

Bevin, sorry I couldn't talk before. R U still up?

I stare at my phone waiting for a text back, but I don't get one.

Lucy's tip for becoming a better person:
Apologize when you know you need to, and even
sometimes when you don't think you need to.

The next morning I sleep really late. When my
eyes finally open, it's after ten.

I'm upstairs washing my face and getting dressed when I
hear my phone ring. Maybe it's Sunny calling to apologize. I
let it go to voice mail and then I wait and wait and wait for
the message. Nothing. Finally I check my missed calls and see
that it was Yamir.

Now I'm stuck in that weird place not knowing if I should
call him back or just ignore it.

Ten minutes later, the phone rings again. It's Yamir.

"Hello."

"I thought you'd never answer," he says.

"Oh. Sorry." I laugh, but I have no idea why.

"Wanna come to Great Escape today? Me, Clint, Anthony,
maybe Sunny and Evan are all going."

I don't know what to say. "Um, I really can't, Yamir. I feel like I need to be at the spa so people take me seriously."

Right after I say it, I regret it. I can go. I know I can. No one cares if I'm at the spa. No one wants me to be at the spa, even though I hate admitting that to myself.

"You never want to do anything anymore, Luce-Juice."

"Don't say that." I start doodling on my desk blotter. Sometimes it helps me think more clearly. My thoughts are spiraling around in my head and I feel like I don't have control over what I'm going to say next. "Anyway, I heard you think that girl Arianna is really pretty. Why don't you invite her to Great Escape?"

"Huh?"

"That's what Sunny said." I should stop talking. I know I should. But I can't. "She said you were talking to Clint about her."

"You're crazy, Lucy," Yamir says, all disgusted-sounding. "And anyway, I'm tired of asking you to do things and you saying no."

"That's not true. I did the hot-dog-eating contest."

"I gotta go. And we leave tomorrow to visit my cousins in L.A." I hear the dinging sounds of his video game starting up in the background. "So I guess I'll see you around."

He hangs up.

Maybe I have been saying no a lot, but not all the time. I did the hot-dog-eating contest. And the other things weren't my fault. I had Bevin to deal with and all the stuff at the spa. He should be able to understand that.

I take one more look in the mirror before I head downstairs and notice I have a billion new freckles on the bridge of my nose and on my cheeks. That's pretty much the best sign of a good summer, except so much of this summer hasn't been good at all. I don't get how that's possible, but it just seems to be the way it is.

"Ready to go?" Claudia asks me when I'm downstairs.

"Yup."

"What's wrong, Lucy?"

"Nothing. I'm fine."

Claudia walks closer to me. "Yeah, right. I know you. You're my little sister. I can tell how you're feeling. And you're definitely not fine."

"I'm fine!" I shout, and run outside.

I wait for them by the side of the car.

She's right. I'm not fine. I know I'm not fine. My best friend hates me and my almost-boyfriend doesn't want to be my almost-boyfriend anymore. Even my makeover project, Bevin, hasn't called me back. I'm not even allowed to help at the spa I helped create.

I am so not fine. And all I want is to be fine again. I just don't know how to get there.

When I get to the pharmacy, I try to just lie low and organize some shelves and stay out of everyone's way. I have to admit that I'm a little nervous about Bevin. If she hasn't called, she must be really upset, and if she's upset, Gary is too, and if I could make myself invisible right now, I would.

As soon as I hear the stairs from the upstairs apartment creaking, I make myself as busy as possible, taking all the shampoo bottles off the shelf and then putting them back up as neatly as I can.

"Lucy. We need to talk," Bevin says, standing behind me.

My project is backfiring. I'm regretting my decision to give Bevin a personality and life-skills makeover. Suddenly she's bold and confident and I'm about to be in huge trouble.

"OK, let's go over here, Bevin," I whisper, and guide her to the Relaxation Room. Unfortunately, there's a group of middle-aged ladies in there discussing the college application process. "Let's go outside. I changed my mind."

Once we're outside, I take a deep breath. "First of all, I'm really—"

Bevin interrupts me. "No, I talk first. You totally ditched me. I barely know Annabelle and them and I thought you were going to meet me," she yells. "And then they started prank-calling people in the grade, and they made me do it too. And I don't even know these people!"

People on the sidewalk are watching us have this conversation and I think it's bad for business. We need to look happy and relaxing.

"Bevin, I'm sorry, I thought you were OK to go on your own. And then I had to go to this meeting, and time got away from me."

"What meeting?"

Uh-oh. Suddenly I realize I shouldn't tell her about the business owners' group. I don't know how to get out of this one.

"Oh, just Earth Club stuff, really, no big deal."

"Yeah, that's another thing those girls were saying—you like projects. The way you made Sunny more confident when she liked Evan Mass, and how you're now obsessed with making the school green, and of course all the stuff with Old Mill Pharmacy. They said the only reason you're helping me is because I'm a project." She pauses and sniffles a bit. "Not because you really care about me."

My throat goes lumpy. "Bevin, that's not true at all. I . . . um . . . of course I care about you."

"Well, you say that now, but when I called you last night, you couldn't even talk to me, and it took you forever to call me back." She sniffles again. "Forget it, Lucy. I know the truth. You never liked me. You just needed a project because no one really wanted you involved in the spa opening."

Wow. That was harsh. I created a monster. I succeeded in turning Bevin confident and social, but now she's also really mean.

Bevin folds her arms across her chest. "Let's just take a break on the life makeover, OK? And maybe also a break from each other."

I don't respond.

"Bye, Lucy." She walks away before I have a chance to say anything else.

Lucy's tip for a great summer:

When it's too hot to be outside, go to the movies to be in the air-conditioning and get a supersized fountain soda.

The next few days feel like walking through cotton candy. The air is so sticky hot that it's hard to breathe or even be outside for a minute. The only way to stay outdoors is to stay in the pool the entire time.

Sunny and Yamir are off in Los Angeles. I haven't heard from them at all, except for a text from Sunny at the airport saying good-bye and that our favorite book series is front and center at the airport bookstore.

Gary signed Bevin up for some kind of sailing camp. Apparently he didn't want her hanging around the store so much. Which really means he didn't want her hanging around me so much.

I'm a pariah. No one wants to be near me. Sad, but true.

I guess the one needing a life makeover is me. And as soon as I figure out where to start, I will.

Anais is constantly running around dealing with the inspection. I thought it would have been dealt with already, but apparently not.

The funny thing is, all the people from that small business owners' group have been e-mailing nonstop about inspection problems. That woman Ruthie is apparently the guru and knows how to fix just about any inspection issue, though. So they're lucky to have her.

Some of the new spa employees have already started working, and they have a few appointments each day. It's more like an orientation, since the spa can't totally open until after the inspection is complete. They seem nice enough, but I don't really feel close to them yet.

Even though I was pretty much told to stay out of official spa business, I still check the e-mails a few times a day. When a new e-mail comes in I write the appointment down in the official appointment book and I send the customer a confirmation e-mail.

No one's asked who's doing it. Maybe they forget to check the e-mails. But I like doing it, and this way I'm at least doing something.

I've also been writing back and forth with Sarabeth, the stressed-out bride, making sure all of her appointments are in order. She has eight bridesmaids and they're all getting hair and makeup, plus her mom, her mother-in-law, and four grandmothers. That's a lot of appointments, so even if they're the only people who book for the grand opening, we're still in good shape.

"Yoo-hoo. Anyone here?" I hear someone saying. I don't recognize the voice right away.

I peek my head out from the spa reception area and see that it's Mayor Danes. His chief of staff, Amelia, is with him, wearing a pencil skirt and white blouse. It's really kind of amazing she's not sweating through it. I guess she's the kind of person who never sweats.

"Hi!" I say, and walk over to them.

"Oh, hello, Lucy!" Mayor Danes shakes my hand and I suddenly feel very official. "You're just the girl I wanted to see."

"I am?"

He nods. "Yessiree. I am working on the official press release for the grand opening. Can you believe it's in two weeks?"

I shake my head. I need to see a calendar. I wonder if we're really even ready to open this spa in two weeks.

"Well, I want to make sure I have everything correct, and I'd love to get a few quotes from you," he says. "Also, I know you're working on the Going Green proposal for the Old Mill School Board and I'd love to work that in." He smiles a big politician's smile.

"OK."

"I can't miss an opportunity to highlight our wonderful schools," he adds. "Amelia's going to record this so we have everything correct. Where should we go sit down?"

"Um." I look around. I don't see anyone. That hasn't happened in a long time. "Let's go to the spa office. It's all new and beautiful."

I'm surprised Mayor Danes didn't make this all official and set it up with Anais or my grandma in advance. I'm surprised he isn't asking to talk to them. But I'm not complaining!

We walk slowly into the spa area and I casually look around to make sure no one's there. But it's totally empty and quiet. I wonder if Anais called a special meeting and left me out on purpose. It sounds like I'm being paranoid, but that's totally something she would do.

I can't believe how amazing I thought she was in the beginning. She's one of those people who make a great first impression and that's it.

"Ready?" Mayor Danes asks Amelia.

"Yes, sir!" she says in a jokey voice. She always looks very official and serious, but she can be funny too. I like that. She hits the RECORD button on her iPad, and I start picking my cuticles out of nervousness.

"So," Mayor Danes starts. "I know the whole story behind this wonderful spa, but will you please refresh my memory?"

I smile. Mayor Danes is such a kind man. I bet he could be president if he wanted to. He'd get the Republicans and the Democrats to get along really well just because he's so nice. Sometimes I wonder if the secret to doing well in life is just being nice. Being nice and doing the right thing, and that's it.

Right then as I'm talking about the whole idea behind the spa and everything that happened, I realize that there are a few things I have to do. I need to be more like Mayor Danes. I need to always know the right thing, and if I don't know it, then I need to try to figure it out. Sometimes you need to be the bigger person and apologize even if you've been hurt too. Sometimes you need to really try to put yourself in someone else's position.

As soon as I'm done with this interview, I need to do the right thing.

"And tell me how the Earth Club at Old Mill Middle School influenced your work at your family's pharmacy," he says. One of his legs is crossed over the other and I notice that he has purple socks on.

He catches me staring at them and he says, "Oh, I always wear purple socks." He laughs. "You never noticed before?"

I shake my head.

"Yup. I made a bet with a student once. If he did his homework and got at least a B for the year, I'd wear purple socks every single day."

"Really?" I ask. "You were a teacher?"

He nods. "Yup. For ten years."

It makes sense that Mayor Danes was a teacher, because he really cares about people, especially kids. He thinks kids can do as much as adults can. "So I really started going to Earth Club because of my best friend, Sunny. Her mom made her go and she wanted me to go with her, and so I did and that changed everything."

I hope he doesn't include the mom-making-her-go part in the press release, but I can't exactly tell him what to include and what not to include. But as I'm talking, I realize that so much of what has happened at the pharmacy and with the spa is because of Sunny. Maybe she's right. Maybe I did take her for granted.

It's funny, but right now it feels like I just keep having epiphany after epiphany. It's like this conversation with Mayor Danes is shedding light on all these issues in my life.

I know he used to be a teacher, but maybe he used to be a psychologist too. Or maybe he's just a really good listener and he asks the right questions.

When we finish with the official interview part we sit talking, and he tells me all about his daughter who is a Rhodes scholar studying in London and his son who opened a gluten-free bakery in Seattle.

"I'm so proud of them," he says. "They're good kids. They really know—"

Our conversation is interrupted by shouts. Familiar-sounding shouts. My mom and grandma fighting. It's weird, though, because I haven't heard them yelling like this in a really long time.

"I told you to handle the paperwork," Grandma says. "I told you we needed an extra set of eyes!"

"I did! I did!" Mom's screaming and running behind Grandma as she walks through the pharmacy. Luckily I don't see any customers, since it's pretty early in the day.

"Jane! Doris!" I see Anais running behind them too, and without meaning to, I burst out laughing. It's ridiculous to see three grown woman running through the store like maniacs with their hands in the air. It's not like they have to chase the paperwork before it gets away.

"Um, maybe you should go," I whisper to Mayor Danes and Amelia. "I'm sure everything's fine, but you know how it is, it gets stressful when you're trying to open a business."

He nods. "OK, let's keep this as our secret. Not the press release, but that I witnessed all the screaming and running." He smiles. "I don't want to embarrass anyone."

See what I mean? He's so nice. He just does the right thing.

"We'll sneak out this side door," he whispers, and then gathers all his stuff. "See you soon, Lucy. And again, I'm so proud of you. And so impressed."

After they leave, I peek my head out from the spa area and see Mom, Grandma, Anais, and Gary lurking near the pharmacy office.

"Jane, you were the one who was responsible for dotting all the i's and crossing all the t's," Grandma says with her hands on her hips. "I am holding you responsible."

"Mom. Relax." My mom puts a hand on Grandma's shoulder. "I was looking it over, but these snafus happen all the time. Right, Anais?"

I'm having trouble getting the whole picture of their conversation, so I move out of the spa area and into the pharmacy. Anais has her arms across her chest. She's breathing heavily.

"They do happen all the time." She pauses and looks at the floor. "But I hate to tell you this, guys—the person I've been working with has left for vacation. It seems we're not going to have the paperwork in order to open Labor Day weekend."

"What?" Grandma says, more like an exclamation than a question.

"I'm so sorry. I'm so sorry." Anais is sniffling. "This is my fault. I should have stayed on top of it. I'm so sorry." Then she runs out of the pharmacy.

"Gary?" Grandma looks at him with her eyebrows raised. "Any ideas?"

He exhales out of the side of his mouth in this over-the-top exasperated way. "Dor, here's the thing. We can still do the ribbon cutting and the hoopla, and just postpone appointments."

Is he serious? What about Sarabeth? If we cancel, her mom will kill her. And it's her wedding day. That can't happen. I'm about to open my mouth to tell them that when I get a feeling like I should stay quiet. It seems my yelling will only make things worse.

Mom, Gary, and Grandma stand there looking at each other and I go back into the spa area. Anais told all the spa employees to take the rest of the day off since we didn't have any appointments and technically they're not legally allowed to work in the spa yet.

I go back to the computer to make sure Sarabeth didn't have any other questions. There's another appointment request from someone named Palmer Simone.

What a cool name. I open it up.

Hello! I know it's last-minute, but I'm in charge of the bachelorette/shower for my sister Walker. She, her six bridesmaids, and I are staying at the Old Mill Inn over Labor Day weekend. We'd love to get facials and massages at Pink & Green and bring in drinks and food. I'm wondering if it's possible for us to rent out the spa area for Saturday night. Let me know.

Thank you,

Palmer Simone

That would be great for business. And it wouldn't take away from other appointments since it's at night, but I can't answer her now because I don't know if we'll be allowed to do it. I'll keep the message as new and get back to her as soon as I can.

I click back over to my personal e-mail, where there are tons more back-and-forth discussion e-mails from the small business owners' group. I really don't have time to look at it now. But there's also an e-mail from my dad.

Hey Lu-ney Tune,

The countdown is on! Four days until I see you. I'm taking a cab from the airport and I'll pick you and Claud up at the house for a day of fun and surprises before the wedding. We got an e-mail last week. Get this—they're apparently only serving raw food for most of the wedding. Yuck. OK, love you.

See you soon.

Dad

A day of fun and surprises? Normally I'd go crazy trying to figure out what he's planning. I'd ask Sunny what she thinks and we'd come up with all these elaborate plans like a hot-air balloon ride to New York City and then a Broadway show and shopping spree at FAO Schwarz and sushi at Morimoto and a hot-air balloon ride back.

But I don't have time to come up with elaborate plans now. I have work to do. I have to figure out how I can get this spa opening back on track. I can't cancel on Sarabeth after we bonded on the Fourth of July and she confided in me. And the bachelorette party for Palmer's sister sounds amazing and fun. I want to make that happen.

I can't just sit at a computer and think. I need to literally be touching the keys or reading something. It helps my brain process. So I read articles online and check back through the spa e-mail to see if I've missed anything and then I go back to my personal e-mail to see if Yamir or Sunny e-mailed me anything from L.A.

Nothing in either account.

All I have to read is the boring business group e-mails about things I don't really understand. But I hate seeing all those new e-mails highlighted in my in-box. I like to have everything clean, showing that all is read and I don't have any new messages. So I click through them and skim them, looking for coupons and discounts that some of the businesses offer for group members and friends of group members. Maybe if the grand opening of our spa falls apart, I can send Sarabeth and Palmer to another spa in the group. I guess that wouldn't be the worst thing ever.

Outside in the pharmacy, I hear Grandma helping a customer with one of our custom gift baskets. The customer wants to take all these fancy bath products over to her friend who just had a baby.

Mom's on the phone in the pharmacy office. I can't hear everything she's saying, but it's probably about the inspection or a story for the *Old Mill Observer*. She takes her sort-of staff writer position very seriously, even though it's not even full-time.

I wonder if Anais is at her apartment now, packing up, ready to go somewhere else. Or what if she loses her job all together because she messed up everything for Pink & Green?

Yeah, she got a little crazy after a while, and she didn't

really want me involved with anything, but she's good at her job. I just wanted her to like me and to realize that I knew what I was talking about. I didn't want her to get fired.

I'm reading through more of the business owners' group e-mails, all this stuff about misfiled paperwork, and certain forms needing stamps, and other forms needing to be clipped and not stapled, and that's when it occurs to me. I don't know why it took so long. Sometimes forcing myself to figure things out isn't necessary when the answer is really right in front of me.

Sometimes if you just open your eyes and calm down, you realize all the resources you have right at your fingertips.

I've just had so many epiphanies, I almost don't know what to do first.

"I'm going to do research for Earth Club," I call out to the pharmacy as I'm leaving. I don't want to get into a lengthy conversation with Mom and Grandma where they ask where I'm going, so instead, I just run out of the store. If they really need me or get worried, they can call me on my cell phone.

It seems like God is looking out for me, because Ruthie volunteers at the southeastern Connecticut food co-op a few days a week, and this just so happens to be one of the days she's there. I wonder if she knows my mom. My mom used to work here back in the day before she got so fed up with the people. All they did was sit around and talk about all these amazing things they were doing, but they never actually did anything.

Instead of stocking shelves or bagging groceries, they'd just sit there talking about how amazing it is to use cloth diapers. Finally my mom got so mad she quit.

I wonder if Ruthie's one of those sit-around-and-talk-instead-of-doing people. I doubt it.

"Louise!" Ruthie yells as she sees me coming in. I guess she recognizes me even without the sari on. The co-op is walking distance from the pharmacy, but it's over a hundred degrees, so I'm dripping with sweat when I get there. "Let me get you some water."

It turns out Ruthie is one of the managers, so she's allowed to go in the back office and talk. She guides me there and hands me a jar, like an old cleaned-out pickle jar, full of water with a lemon slice. Some people love to use jars for glasses. It's kind of cool, and very green—reusing the jars is better than throwing them away!

"How can I help?" Ruthie pulls her frizzy gray curls into a tortoiseshell clip, which makes it look like she's ready for business.

I debated the whole way over whether or not I should tell Ruthie my real name and admit that I lied. I decided I had to come clean. I need real help here.

It was probably wrong of me to lie, but I hope Ruthie understands why I did it.

I tell her the whole story, about the pharmacy and the spa and Anais and the inspection.

She smiles this calming grown-up smile and sits back in her chair. "I know who you are, Lucy. I knew the whole time."

"Really?"

"Yes." She smiles. "Your mother and I go way back. She's a doll."

I should've figured, but somehow it was easier to be Louise Ramal for a little while. Sometimes you need to pretend a little bit to get where you want to be. It's like that saying: "Fake it till you make it." If you act like you belong, you will be treated that way. It doesn't really make sense, but it's just the way it is.

"Here's what you need to do," Ruthie says, leaning forward in her chair. "Go find Anais, get all the paperwork you can, every single thing even if you think it's not necessary, especially the forms from the inspector. Then come back here."

"Please don't call my mom or grandma," I say, suddenly worried. "I don't want to involve them. You'd think they'd believe me by now that I can handle things and help things, but for some reason they don't."

"Lucy, here's one thing you should remember," Ruthie says softly. "In some people's eyes, you will always be a kid. It's just how it is. And you will grow to appreciate it."

Ruthie's one of those people who has a calming presence.

She could be talking about the country's deficit and how much in debt we are to China, and it would seem calming.

"OK. I'll try to remember that."

"It's going to work out," she tells me.

I stand up. "Thank you so much."

"You're very welcome. Good luck."

It feels like a billion degrees, like I'm walking through a fire pit in a fur coat, but I start running anyway. Anais's apartment is about a mile from the co-op, but I can do it. I throw my backpack over my shoulders and put my hair up in a high bun and I run. I run and run and run and I'm huffing and puffing and worried I may pass out on the sidewalk, but I keep running. It feels good. I suddenly understand why people who love running talk about it all the time. It feels like I'm literally releasing all the stress and frustration into the air and it's leaving me and hopefully won't ever come back.

I finally get to Anais's apartment complex. Before I ring her bell, I go out on the beach and breathe in the salty sea air. There's something about ocean air that makes all of your problems seem small. The salty smell and the view of the ocean and the waves make every problem seem fixable. Everything can be solved, if you take a few minutes to look at the ocean before dealing with it.

I can't let any more time slip away, so I walk into Anais's

apartment building and tell the doorman that I know her and that I can just go up and ring the bell. I don't want the doorman to call up to her in case she doesn't let me up.

The doorman agrees and I go to the elevator and push floor number five, and then I walk to her apartment. I use the silver knocker, and after a few seconds, Anais comes to the door.

"Lucy," she says with a hint of surprise.

"Hi, Anais, I know you don't really like me, but can I come in for a minute? I think I can help."

She sighs. "I never said I didn't like you, Lucy."

I probably shouldn't have said that.

"Come in."

I walk in slowly, expecting to find boxes all over the place. But her apartment looks just as lovely as it did when I was there over the Fourth of July. Maybe she's not running away as fast as I thought she was.

"Would you like some lemonade? Water? It's so hot." Anais has a ceiling fan going and the door to the balcony open and it actually feels so lovely and cool. I can hear the ocean. If I were her, I'd sleep with the windows open every single night.

"Lemonade would be great," I tell her. When she's in the kitchen, I sit back on her couch and look out the window and

I imagine myself living here as a grown-up. I'd throw dinner parties and we'd play board games and go for late-night swims in the pool and the ocean.

"So," she says when she gets back to the couch with the lemonade.

"Here's the thing. I'll make it quick," I start, and then take a second to collect my thoughts. I don't want it to seem like I know better than Anais, because I obviously don't. I just know this one thing. "A few weeks ago I snuck out to this Connecticut and Rhode Island small business owners' meeting because . . . well, I just felt like I wanted to be a part of things, and I didn't know how to be. When I was there, I met this woman, Ruthie, who runs the group. She can handle any inspection problem, and so I came to talk to you and we can collect the papers, and um, she can help us." I decide it's time to stop talking. I've probably already said too much.

"Lucy, that's very sweet of you," she says, and I'm waiting for the "but," the reason why it won't work and I should give up trying right now.

"So you'll do it?" I ask.

"Do what?"

"I mean, um, you'll listen to me, and we can organize the paperwork and then go back to Ruthie and then, um, see what happens?" I'm rambling and can't seem to stop. Maybe it's the sugary lemonade going to my head, or the relaxing salty ocean air breeze.

"Sure. Whatever you think." Anais smiles. "Everything got crazy back there. I really love your family and your pharmacy and the spa, and I want things to work out for the grand opening Labor Day weekend. So if you know of a way to help, it can't hurt to try."

"Great!" I jump up and move to hug her, and it feels like such a relief that I didn't have to battle it out with her. She just listened to me, and believed me, and has faith that I can help.

It's that whole bring-your-own-chair philosophy. If you just go into it, and bring everything you've got, people will trust you eventually.

"We're going to need to go back to the spa, though, and grab all the files," Anais tells me. "I'm not sure what your mom or grandma will think."

It occurs to me that maybe Anais is nervous to see them after the whole argument. I'm nervous to see them too, and I haven't done anything wrong.

"You're right." I stop to think for a second, wondering if maybe they have plans and they'll be out somewhere. I doubt it. They rarely have plans.

I text Claudia to see what's going on at the store. I realize I didn't even see her before I left.

Hey claud. What r u up to?

A few seconds later, she texts me back.

Mom, Grandma and I r @ Sil's to look for a dress
4 Mom 4 Esme's wedding. U @ earth club still?

I totally forgot! Today was the big shopping day. My mom hates shopping, so she had to make this whole big production of scheduling a day when we could go with her to find a dress. Sil's is this boutiquey shop in North Mill and it's the only place my mom shops. I was supposed to go with them and they must think I bailed for Earth Club. Oh well.

Yup. So sorry I forgot. Get Mom something
good! Xo

"OK, coast is clear," I tell Anais. "They're all out shopping. I guess Tory and Charise are covering the store. Who knows where Gary is, but he's so oblivious, I bet he won't even notice us in the spa getting the files."

"He is really oblivious, right?" Anais laughs. "I must've asked him thirty times to go over all the order forms and invoices and he was barely paying attention." She stops talking for a second, and dabs on some lip balm. "Not that I'm placing blame."

"Yeah, he's a scatterbrain. My mom is too. That's why they can't get along." I laugh. I don't know why I'm sharing these family secrets with Anais, but it seems like it's easing the tension.

"I think Gary's in love with your mom," Anais adds, and then covers her mouth. "Oops. I've said too much."

I crack up. "No, it's OK. It's never gonna happen. He's been in love with her for years. My dad's coming back in a few days and going to a wedding with my mom. They were invited separately; they're still good friends with this woman Esme they knew in college. She's seriously a crazy person, but they stay friends. I don't know why."

Anais nods. "My parents are divorced too. I get it."

"Oh, they're not divorced," I add. "Just separated. They get along. I've heard them on the phone and stuff."

Anais nods again. I know what she's thinking. That I have all this false hope and I should get over the idea that they're going to get back together. I've seen that nod and that expression from a million people before. I don't care, though. I still have hope. I think it can happen.

Lucy's tip for a great summer:

Walk along a boardwalk as often as you can.

I'm glad you made up with Bevin," Anais says as we're in a cab on the way back to the pharmacy. She gets to take cabs back and forth since she doesn't have a car and her company pays all expenses. It's a really nice life, if you ask me.

"I didn't make up with her yet," I say, confused. "I've been planning out exactly what I want to say. I totally messed up."

"She told me you did." Anais gives me a crooked smile and I'm not really sure what it means. "She said you apologized and you went out for ice cream at 384 Sprinkles and then got manicures or something?"

I giggle nervously. "That sounds fun, but it didn't actually happen."

"The manicure part seemed a little iffy, since you guys practically live in a spa that just hired manicurists." Anais

215

laughs too. Even this story is really funny, I'm not sure what I should do about it.

"She just wants to be your friend, Lucy," Anais adds after a few minutes of awkward silence with only the cab's eighties music station breaking the tension.

"Yeah. I know. I was actually starting to like her."

"I guess she made up that whole story because that's what she wishes would happen," Anais says. "But she'll be leaving soon anyway, to go back to Manhattan, right?"

I nod. "Yeah, I guess right after Labor Day."

"Today's the last day of her sailing camp," Anais tells me.

"I'll make up with her," I say. "For real this time."

The cab lets us out right in front of the pharmacy. Inside, I see Tory and Charise helping customers and everything going smoothly even without Grandma or Mom or me there. It's good to know we can all take a break once in a while and not have to worry.

We rush into the spa area and Anais goes straight to the pink filing cabinet behind the reception desk. All of the filing cabinets and supply cabinets are either pink or green, and some are pink-and-green striped. When I think about the time it took to order these supplies, it's amazing we got it done and with a few weeks to spare. The tables are covered with that soft paper, and the towels are rolled up neatly in baskets.

I want the grand opening to be now! I want to greet the customers and I want to welcome them and I want to hear all the compliments about how amazing Pink & Green is.

"Well, this is it." Anais shows me about four folders stuffed full of paper. "It's all organized by date. I have the sign-off from B. Bond, the inspector." She points to the signature and everything.

"If we have the sign-off, what happened? Why aren't we approved or whatever?"

Anais sighs. "Apparently it wasn't filed the right way, and we missed the person who does the filing because he's away the next two weeks." She rolls her eyes. "You'd think anyone could handle the filing, since it's the actual inspection that matters, but it's all red tape."

I still don't understand it, but Ruthie said she could help.

I sit at the spa reception desk while I'm waiting for Anais to finish gathering all the paperwork. I look at the beautiful Pink & Green notepad and business cards that just came in. I love the font on everything—curly and cute and feminine. Mom really did an amazing job with the branding. She even found these pink-and-green-striped gift bags so if people buy products to take home, they're carrying them in style. And the best part is that all our paper stuff is made out of recycled materials; even the gift bags are reusable. We're totally true to our eco-spa mission.

Anais comes back over to me with another folder. "E-mails back and forth," she says. She's wearing an ivory sundress and gold strappy sandals and, truthfully, she should've been the one to take Mom shopping. Anais has the best fashion sense out of any of us.

She's also probably right about Bevin. As soon as this whole inspection thing is taken care of, and Ruthie helps us, I'm going to smooth things over with Bevin.

Slowly but surely I'm checking things off my worry list. Soon all I'll have to worry about is Sunny and Yamir. But they're still in California, and I think a little time away will do all of us good. Besides, I can't fix everything at once!

We're waiting for the cab to pick us up when my phone rings. I told Anais that we could walk to the food co-op from here, but she decided that it's way too hot to walk even a few inches. I pretty much agree with her, especially after running all the way to her apartment.

"Hello?" I say, worried that it's going to be Ruthie telling us not to even bother coming. The number on the caller ID came up as private.

"Luce! Guess what? Mom found an ah-may-zing dress!" Claudia shouts. "Come over here, now. Bean can pick you up!"

"Um." As nice as it is that Claudia thought to call me, I really can't just drop everything and go over there right now. "I can't, actually. But I am so so so so excited about Mom's dress. I'll see it later tonight."

"No. It's going to the tailor for alterations in an hour. You need to see it now."

She's acting a little crazy. "I can't, Claud. You know how important this school board proposal is." I pause and I hear voices in the background, but I can't tell who's talking. I didn't know Sil's was such a popular store. It always seemed like a weird combination of hippie and old lady to me.

"Lucy! Seriously. Just come. Bean will get you at school in ten minutes. Finish up." She's talking with a list of instructions and commands, not suggestions. She's talking like I don't have a choice.

"I can't. Also, my phone's dying. I gotta go. Love you."

I hang up and exhale and pray that Bean doesn't just show up at school.

"What was that all about?" Anais asks, startling me. For a second, I forgot she was even there.

"My sister was insisting that I go over to this boutique to see a dress my mom bought for that wedding this weekend." I brush some sweat off my forehead. "I don't get why it's such a big deal. It's not like it's her best friend's wedding or anything. They talk once a year."

Thinking about that makes me sad. What if that's what happens to Sunny and me one day? What if we become busy grown-ups who only have time to talk once a year? We talk pretty much once an hour now—or at least, we did before our fight—so it would really have to be seriously bad to turn into once a year. I try to brush that worry away. There's no way that will ever happen.

The cab pulls up and we get in, and thankfully the air-conditioning is going at its highest speed. It's a three-minute drive, so we're there in a flash and the driver doesn't even charge us. He drives Anais around all the time, so he says he'll get us on the next ride.

Claudia keeps calling me and I keep hitting IGNORE. I don't get it. It's like when she wants me, I have to be there in a second. But when she doesn't, or when she's busy with Bean or college, she totally forgets I exist. I wish we could find some kind of middle ground.

Also, it's really kind of sad that all Mom, Grandma, and Claudia care about is this dress when we have an inspection to worry about. They don't even care that the spa may not open, after all our hard work. It doesn't make sense.

Ruthie's waiting for us at the front of the co-op. She leads us toward the office. "Have a seat, ladies," she tells us. "I'm going to call my friend Patch and I think he'll know exactly what to do."

It's hard to believe I was just here a few hours earlier. It feels like that was weeks ago. It's only three o'clock, but it feels like midnight.

"Hey, Patch, it's Ruthie," she says into the phone. I like when people use the nickname Patch for guys named Patrick. It sounds so cute. "Yup, got another one. Uh-huh. I'll hold."

She puts the phone on speaker, sits back in her rolling chair, and says to us, "I see on your forms that it was Brandon Bond who did your inspection. He's an OK guy, but he's messed up the filing many times. That's why you're in trouble."

I wait for her to say more, but she doesn't. I wonder if our "trouble" is the kind of trouble that can be solved. Or not.

"After you talk to Patrick, what can we do? I mean, what's the next step?" Anais asks. "I've been in this business for fifteen years, opened spas in fifteen states, but I've never run into the kind of nitty-gritty I have here."

Ruthie nods. "I know. So many balls in the air." She types something into her computer and looks back at us.

"I didn't get the whole story here," Anais says. "Which spa is yours? Is it the Green Oasis in Ferry Port or the Dove and Canary in South Brookfield?"

Ruthie laughs. "Actually, we just sold our spa a few weeks ago. We're in the process of opening a bed-and-breakfast."

Anais nods, and Patrick comes back on the line. Ruthie picks up the phone and takes him off speaker.

"Right." She pauses. "Yes, they have." Pause again. "Yes, they have done everything, with ample time, every form is filled out in beautiful handwriting." She smiles at Anais. "I have it right here." Ruthie makes a face as if Patrick is talking too much, and she has her finger holding a spot on a piece of paper, like she doesn't want to lose what she was looking for. "Yes, it's dhg3727883mag." She takes a deep breath and gives us two thumbs-up. "Thank you so much, Patch. You always come through for me. But you need to talk to Brandon about why he's making so many mistakes." She claps quietly. "Right. OK, take care, Patch. Have a great rest of the summer."

Ruthie hangs up and exhales again. She goes to fill a few drinking jars with this organic sparkling apple juice. She hands a jar to Anais and one to me. "Cheers, ladies!" We clink jars. "You did it."

"You did it!" I yell. "Ruthie, you saved the day."

"Well, Louise Ramal, I think *you* saved the day."

I smile, and Anais looks at me, confused. I don't feel like explaining the whole name thing—that can be my private joke with Ruthie. I have a feeling we'll keep in touch.

We stay and chat with Ruthie for a few minutes, and then Ruthie has to go do a shift shelving produce. Anais wants to get back to the apartment and shower before meeting everyone back at the spa later this evening.

"Shouldn't you be getting to Sil's?" Anais asks.

"I doubt they're still there," I tell her. "I'll go back to the pharmacy and tidy the shelves and wait for them."

Anais calls the cab again (I swear, she refuses to walk anywhere, I don't get how she stays so thin), and the driver drops me off at the pharmacy before he drops her off at her apartment.

I walk in, and there's a line of customers behind the pharmacy counter. Charise is handling their purchases. Everyone seems happy, though, and a few people are waiting in the Relaxation Room. All the lights are off in the spa area. I wave hi to Charise and Tory and walk around making sure the shelves are nice and neat, the way Grandma likes them. Everything looks perfect.

But I don't see any of my family anywhere. They can't all still be at Sil's—it's not that big or interesting of a store. I decide to go to the pharmacy office to play on the computer until they get back. Maybe they went out for a snack.

As I get closer to the office, I hear voices—Mom's, Grandma's, Claudia's, and a male voice. It's hard to hear well with all the customers chatting and laughing, but I'm pretty sure it's not Bean's voice that I'm hearing.

I hurry back and push the door open.

"Luney-Tune!"

My dad is here! My dad is here!

Right then all of my doubts and anger and frustration melt away like the last few seconds of a lit candle. He's here and that's all that matters.

"I thought you weren't coming until tomorrow!" I yell, and run into him, practically knocking him down with the force of my hug.

"Surprise!"

"You're here. You're really here. Really and truly here."

"Yeah, Luce." Claudia hits my arm, while I'm still hugging Dad. "We wanted to surprise you at Sil's and all go out for lobster rolls and chowder for lunch, but you were not where you said you were."

Mom's smile quickly changes to a grimace, like she just remembered she was mad at me. "Yes, young lady. Where were you? Why did you lie?" She pats the chair next to her. "Sit. Then spill."

"And Lucy, I know you're happy your father is here, but this is a serious discussion," Grandma adds. "How can we trust you to work at the spa when we don't know where you are?"

I can't believe this is happening. Everyone's ruining my amazing moment with my dad. But I guess I can understand why. I was shady on the phone and then I stopped answering calls and texts. This is my chance to really live my do-the-right-thing philosophy. I was wrong and I need to own up to that.

"Nowhere. She's run away," Bean says, walking into the office.

And then he sees me. He raises a fist in the air. "There you are!" He's laughing, so I know he's not that mad. I don't think Bean really gets mad. "I thought you got hired as the entertainment on a cruise line! Or joined the circus! Or opened your own spa!" He winks at me. "I was worried sick!"

Everyone cracks up, and Dad says, "I like this guy."

I like him too. I just don't want to say it out loud.

"I was keeping my location a secret," I start.

"Of course you were," Grandma interrupts. "Always up to something, my granddaughter." She smiles, so I know she's not really mad. Just a little bit.

"I solved the problem with the inspection," I tell them.

"Lucy," my mom says in her what-have-you-done-now tone.

"No, really, I did," I say. "Ask Anais. It's a whole long story, but basically I know someone who knows someone at the state office who helped us. We passed the inspection with flying colors, the paperwork was just misfiled. It was a whole big misunderstanding. All someone named Brandon's fault."

Grandma looks confused. "But it's all set? Anais will tell me we're all set to open in a week?"

"Yup."

Dad high-fives me, and then everyone starts high-fiving.

"Lucy saved the day again," Claudia says.

"Seems to me Lucy's always the one who saves the day," Bean adds.

"I like you, Bean." I high-five him again.

It was the right time to say it out loud.

Lucy's tip for a great summer:
Build sand castles, but don't worry
if they get knocked down.

Claudia, Bean, Dad, and I spend all of Thursday together. We go out for the famous egg and cheese sandwiches at Amity Deli, right on the beach. And then we play in the sand for hours, like we did when we were little. Dad builds these intricate sand castles that have all these different chimneys and additions and even windows. We of course have lobster rolls for lunch and have a root-beer-drinking contest. Bean wins, but I came close. Bean drank ten huge cups of root beer. I had eight and a half.

And soon it's time for us to head back to the house so that Dad and Mom can leave for Esme's wedding. It's at this holistic yoga center in the middle of New Hampshire. They're both terrible with directions, so they'll probably get lost. It's a good thing they're leaving early, or they'd miss the wedding.

"We all have to do yoga tonight when we get there," Mom says, when we're back and sitting in the living room.

"Everyone?" Dad asks. "What if we don't even like yoga?"

"It's required," Mom says. "There's a whole schedule of activities."

"This is crazy," Dad says, and Mom shakes her head. They're complaining, but deep down they're excited to be going somewhere different together. I can just tell.

"Well, you kids have fun," Grandma says. "Tell Esme I say hello."

"Will do," Dad replies.

"But when you get back, it's crunch time." Grandma looks at Mom. "We'll have five days until the grand opening and that's it. We'll practically be sleeping at the store."

"Ma, we're not in bad shape," Mom tells Grandma. "Take a look around, everything's organized. We need to get in touch with Mayor Danes about the official ribbon cutting and all the hoopla, but as far as appointments and everything, we're doing great."

Grandma raises her eyebrows. "If you say so . . ."

"I say so!" I exclaim, and everyone laughs.

Soon Mom and Dad are off in Mom's old Volkswagen, heading toward New Hampshire. It's hard for me to believe that they're going away for a whole weekend together. Yeah, they weren't officially divorced, and they didn't fight a lot, but it's still weird. It's a good thing a lot of other people will be there. It would be super-awkward if they had to spend a whole weekend alone just the two of them.

In a way, I'm jealous that they're leaving, because I only got to see my dad for one full day and a little bit the night before. But in another way, I'm glad that my mom gets to spend time with him. It's hard to say. I guess that's what they mean by mixed feelings.

"So it's just us all weekend," Grandma says, with her feet up on the ottoman. "Bean, what's for dinner?"

"I was thinking Mexican—enchiladas, guacamole, margaritas."

"Sounds good," Grandma says. "Except the last part. No underage drinking in my house."

"Kidding, Doris, kidding."

Grandma smiles. "Make sure there's enough for six. I invited Gary and Bevin over." Grandma looks at me. "You haven't apologized, Lucy. I'm very grateful for your help with the inspection, but Bevin is waiting for an apology. It doesn't matter how good you are at solving problems and saving the day if you're not a nice person. Being nice is most important, you know."

If I had a dollar for every time Grandma has said that to me, I'd be able to buy a spa by myself.

"I know." I walk over and give Grandma a hug. She must've been out by the pool while we were out with Dad. She smells like sunscreen, and I love it. I wish everyone could smell like sunscreen all year long. "I've been planning out exactly what I want to say. I'm sorry it has taken so long."

I run upstairs and throw on my red-and-white polka-dot tankini, grab a towel out of the linen closet, and sprint down the stairs and out the back door to the pool. I set up my towel on the lounge chair, lie back, and take out my phone.

"Bevin?" I say, when I hear someone answer.

"Yeah?"

"Hi, it's Lucy."

"I know."

OK, so she's not going to make this easy for me. That's fine. I deserve it. She ruined my client's makeup way back in the beginning of summer, but I wasn't exactly welcoming to her either, and I waited so long to call and apologize. I've totally been avoiding her.

"Do you want to come swimming before dinner?" I ask.

"Maybe. I'm helping Anais put all of the appointments into the computer."

"Listen, Bevin, it shouldn't have taken me so long to call you. I'm really sorry." I stop to think for a second. "I know you think you were just another one of my projects, but it's not true."

She doesn't say anything and so I take that as a sign to go on. "I like you. I like the way you keep asking questions, like you really care about a person, and you're not just making conversation. I like the way you still fold over your anklet socks like a kid, but you can pull it off and make it look classy and cool. I like the way you're friendly and make people feel like they've known you forever even if they've just met you."

"That's not even true," she mumbles.

"Yes, it is," I tell her.

"You really think I have an easy time making friends?"

"Yes. I do." I clear my throat. "But you have to give yourself a chance. Don't think it's going to happen in five minutes, and don't assume that they're not going to like you, because they will."

"Really really?"

"Yes. Really really."

"Dad! Can I go over to Lucy's and swim?" she yells straight into the phone.

"Sure!" I hear Gary yell back.

"I'll be there in five minutes! Bye!" She hangs up, and I guess that means she accepted my apology.

I jump in the pool and float around, savoring these few minutes of quiet time before Bevin comes over.

As I'm floating, I think about Mom and Dad and the wedding, and the great day Claudia, Bean, and I had with Dad. I think about saving the day with Ruthie. I'm grateful to have a clear head now that I made peace with Bevin. I think about the grand opening and how amazing it's going to be, the ribbon cutting and Sarabeth and all her fancy friends and family getting ready for the wedding. I think about the news crews that will be there, and the paper, and all the boats on the water for Boat Fest.

But something still doesn't feel quite right. I've figured out a lot, but there're two other things I need to figure out.

And they're both named Ramal.

Lucy's tip for becoming a better person:
Be grateful for what you have.

Dinner with Bevin and Gary ends up being pretty nice. Bean makes a Mexican feast and we sit at the table long after we've finished eating, just talking and laughing. And Bevin likes night swimming as much as I do, so we change back into our suits and race out to the pool for a late-night swim.

"You're so lucky to have a pool," she says.

"I know."

"You're so lucky that your parents get along even if they're not together," she says.

"I know."

"And Sunny's a pretty awesome best friend."

"I know."

She keeps listing a million other reasons I'm lucky: I have an older sister, my grandma doesn't need a wheelchair like hers does, I'm allowed to have soda in the house, all this stuff. And as she's talking, I realize that she's right. I really am lucky.

"You get to live in Manhattan, though," I tell her.

"True." She splashes me with water. "But I'd give that up for a private pool."

I splash her back. "Come visit whenever. But it's only open from May to September."

A little while later, Bevin and Gary go home to the pharmacy's upstairs apartment, and it feels funny that they'll be leaving soon and the apartment will be empty again. I wonder if anyone will ever live there in the future. Maybe Claudia and Bean, if they get married one day? That would be cute. I hope I get to be the maid of honor.

Thinking about Claudia's future wedding jogs my memory and I remember something I forgot to do! I'm such an idiot. I race upstairs to the computer. That girl Palmer who's planning her sister's bachelorette party—it's a week away! I totally forgot. I bet they booked another place.

I look through my e-mail and find hers and write her back.

Hello Palmer,

I am so sorry for my delay in responding. We would love to have the bachelorette party at our spa on Saturday evening. Please confirm that you'd still like to have it there.

Thank you,

Lucy Desberg

After I'm done taking care of official spa business, I go downstairs and find Claudia. It's not that late, and there's still something I have to do before tomorrow.

I tap Claudia on the shoulder. She and Bean are watching some documentary about New York City in the early 1900s, but she can be interrupted.

"Can you drive me to Sunny's?" I ask her.

"I thought Sunny was in L.A.," she responds. Sheesh, she has an amazing memory. She has so much going on, and yet she remembers every detail about my friends. That's a nice thing about older sisters.

"She is, but I need to do something."

Claudia looks at me all squinty-eyed and pauses the documentary. "What are you talking about, Lucy?"

"I need to go drop some stuff off. I just need a ride there."

"Claud, come on, let's take her." Bean smiles at me. "Live a little. A few minutes of breaking and entering never hurt anyone!"

He laughs, and I do too, but then I add, "It's not breaking and entering! I know where the key is!"

It only takes me a few minutes to do what I have to do while Bean and Claudia wait in the car.

I put the basket I made right in the middle of Sunny's bed. It's full of all her favorite stuff: pretzel M&M's, Red Hots, hot-dog-flavored potato chips, key-lime-pie-scented lip gloss, her favorite ultra-sheen shampoo, and a package of these new Hello Kitty note cards we just got in at the pharmacy.

I take out a separate card with two artsy-looking ice cream sundaes on the cover and write:

Dear Sunny,

I'm so sorry I have been such an annoying, selfish, weirdo grump this summer. I know this basket of some of your favorite stuff won't totally make up for it, but maybe it's a good start? I love you. I hope we're still BFFs.

A million hugs,
Lucy

Spend as much time with your friends as you can!

My phone rings at seven A.M. the next morning. My eyes are still closed when I answer it, so I don't even see the caller ID.

"We're baaaaaaack," the voice on the other end sings through the phone.

"Sunny! Do you know what time it is?"

She laughs. "Not really. We took the red-eye. I'm all out of whack. Anyway, I couldn't wait any longer."

"For what?"

"To say thank you, duh, for the amazing basket! I love it! And I knew it was a good idea to tell you where we keep the extra key!"

"You're welcome," I mumble, still feeling sleepy. "I'm really sorry. I shouldn't have been so weird about hanging out with AGE, and the Bevin stuff, and leaving you out."

"I'm sorry too!" Sunny yells. "I'm sorry for what happened that day we snuck to Bayberry Cove Library. I'm sorry I said such mean things. And I was talking to Pindar about it, and she said I can't ditch my friends just because I have a boyfriend."

"You and Pindar are getting along again?" I ask. Pindar is Sunny's first cousin on her dad's side, the ones they were just visiting in L.A. She's sixteen and such a know-it-all. They usually fight.

"Yeah, we had the best time together. She's way better now."

"Well, that's good."

"I'm glad we've made up, Lucy. Of course we're still BFFs. I'll be over in forty-five minutes." I hear Yamir and Mr. Ramal arguing about something in the background. "I'm borrowing one of your bathing suits because mine are musty from being in our suitcases."

"OK, I'm going back to sleep until then."

It feels like only five minutes pass before the doorbell rings. I throw myself out of bed to let Sunny in. Grandma's reading the newspaper on the back porch and Bean and Claudia are at the table eating bowls of cereal. Sunny bounds in, practically jumping up and down.

"Sleepyhead! Wake up!"

"Shouldn't you be tired? It's only like six A.M. in Los Angeles right now."

"I'm hyped up! We have a week until the grand opening of Pink and Green."

I smile, and we traipse back up the stairs.

"Come on. Let's swim. And we have to talk," Sunny says when we're back in my room.

"We talked. We forgave each other. Remember?" I take my army-green one-piece out of the drawer and throw it at Sunny. "Here. Borrow this one. Green always looks good on you."

"We have to talk about something else," Sunny says, and goes into the bathroom to change. I run to Claudia's bathroom to brush my teeth and change into my bathing suit. When I get back, Sunny's sitting at my desk, spraying on sunscreen.

"It's about Yamir," she says. She raises her eyebrows up so high, they're practically touching her widow's peak. My heart starts pounding. I bet he fell in love with someone else in L.A. I bet Pindar knew the perfect girl for him. "He really likes you, Lucy. Can you just get it together?"

I try not to show my relief. "Get what together?"

"Just be normal around him." She raises her eyebrows at me again. "I know I was a freak when I started liking Evan, but you told me to stop being dumb, and I did, so I'm telling you the same thing now."

"How do you know he likes me?" I sit down on my bed. "What about that girl Arianna?"

"Oh, that." She pauses and makes a face like she feels bad. "I pretty much made that up because I was annoyed at you. I'm sorry. But he likes you. I overheard him talking to Vishal."

Vishal is their other cousin, Pindar's brother. He's Yamir's age.

"Sun, you're like a super-eavesdropper now!"

"Duh. Who do you think I learned it from?"

I slap her knee. "Fine. I'll try to be more normal around Yamir. But can we just discuss that he's been weird too? He's mean one day and nice the next and he invites me to things and then bails on other plans. Total mixed signals. Right? I think I once heard a song about that."

Sunny nods. "Boys are weird, Lucy. Haven't I said that a million times? That's why we need to stick together."

Sunny and I spend the rest of the day swimming, and she comes out for Chinese food with Grandma, Bean, Claudia, and me. We order Shirley Temples and share chicken chow fun. It feels like old times. Better than old times. She's back, and we've made up, and she told me Yamir likes me. She didn't even bring up Evan once in a way that seemed like she would rather be hanging out with him. We talked about him, but in a fun way.

"Remember what I said," Sunny tells me as we're waiting on the front porch for her mom to pick her up.

"OK. But I don't know what to do about it." I take a small sip of root beer float. Of course we stopped for Dairy Queen on the way home. It is summer, after all.

"Just be Lucy. Don't overthink it."

I'm half hoping Yamir will be in the car when Mrs. Ramal pulls up, but he isn't. Mrs. Ramal waves to me from the driver's seat, and Sunny walks over to the car.

Don't overthink it. I keep hearing that over and over in my head, but it almost seems like an oxymoron. How can you tell your brain not to think? You'd be thinking about not thinking. It's so mind-boggling that it makes me laugh.

I'm like a crazy lady sitting on the front porch drinking a root beer float, laughing by herself, but I don't really mind it.

Lucy's tip for becoming a better person:
Send thank-you notes! Real, handwritten ones.

Dear Lucy,

Thanks so much for getting back to me! We were looking into alternate plans, but the spa was still our first choice! We'll be there around 8 pm. We'd like manicures and pedicures and we'll bring in our own food and drinks. Please get back to me with the price.

Thank you,

Palmer

Grandma went to Block Island with Flo for the day, so I can't ask her the price for renting the spa. So instead, I call Anais and ask her. She's so excited that the spa has already been rented for an evening before it's even officially open that she's really freaking out. "You set this up?" she asks.

"Well, I just responded to the spa e-mail," I tell her.

"Right. I guess I let that slip, after I had to fire our initial receptionist," she says.

"I didn't even know we had a receptionist," I reply, and then wish I hadn't said that. I don't want Anais to think I'm complaining about being left out again.

"Well, tell Palmer it's no charge to rent out the spa, just thirty-five dollars each for manicures and pedicures," Anais decides. "It's a nice little promotion since it's the first weekend and hopefully they'll tell others about it. Let me make sure Denise, Chloe, and Rebecca are all available. They're our best manicurists," she says. "Good work, Lucy."

"Thanks," I say, already typing back to Palmer.

After all of my computer work is done, I realize I forgot to do something very important. Something Mom taught Claudia and me about from a very early age: thank-you notes! I need to write a thank-you note to Ruthie, to thank her for all of her help with the inspection.

I dig around my desk for my best note card and settle on a red card with pencils on the front. I make it short and sweet: thanking her for her help, and encouraging her to come to the grand opening.

When Mom and Dad get back later that evening, they're cracking up as they're walking from the driveway to the house. I don't mean to be spying on them, but I can't help it; I'm on the couch and there's only the screen door between us.

"No one will believe us," Mom says.

"Nope."

"No one will ever understand how awful that was," Mom goes on.

"No, they won't." Dad laughs.

It's weird to see two people saying how awful something was but laughing about it at the same time. It's like they bonded over something horrible. It's pretty funny.

"How was it?" I ask as soon as they open the door.

"Awful," Mom says.

"Don't even ask." Dad laughs again.

"What? Why?" I don't understand how a wedding could really be that awful, but it doesn't seem like they had a fight or anything.

"Let's just put it this way," Mom starts. "We had to do this group chanting exercise to welcome them as husband and wife." She pauses for emphasis. "Then we had to weigh our food waste and participate in trust falls."

"OK, Jane." Dad puts a hand on her shoulder. "Lucy gets it."

Mom leans into him in an exasperated but humored

kind of way, and even though I'm curious about the rest of the wedding weekend, I think I'll wait until everyone else is there to hear it.

"Where's Claudia?" Dad asks.

"Probably in the pool. Where else?"

"Go get her," he says. "Please. And Grandma too."

"Grandma went to Block Island with Flo," I tell them. "She should be back by nine."

They look at each other in this way that seems as if they're speaking with their eyes. I haven't thought about this in so long, but now I remember it—they used to do this all the time when I was little, after I asked them if I could have ice cream or go to an amusement park, stuff like that.

"OK, well, go get Claudia," Dad says.

I practically have to drag Claudia and Bean in from the pool. They throw towels around themselves, but they're dripping water all over the house.

"What was so important?" Claudia asks. "Should we go change?"

"No. Sit." Mom pats the couch next to her.

"Mom, I'm dripping wet," Claudia says snottily.

"It's fine," Mom replies. "It's an old couch."

Bean sits in the leather arm chair, and I realize I'm not

disgusted by his feet. He actually has acceptable feet. His toenails aren't too long, and they're a pretty nice shape.

OK, Lucy, stop. Stop looking at Bean's feet.

"So, we have an announcement to make," Dad starts, and for some reason, my immediate thought is that we're getting a dog. I don't know why. "A lot has been going on for me professionally, and you know I never planned to stay in London forever . . . "

"Australia!" Claudia yells. "Please say Australia! I have always wanted to go to Australia!"

Sheesh, for a smart girl, she's really dumb. Why would we want our dad on the other side of the planet?

"No." Dad laughs. "Not Australia." He stops talking and gives us a look like he's waiting to see if we're ready. "Connecticut."

"What?" I yelp.

"I am now an associate professor of urban planning at Yale University." Dad smiles. "I start in a few weeks."

"Really?" I jump up and run over and hug him. "Really? Really?"

"Really! Really!"

He tells us all about wanting to move on from Oxford, and looking for new opportunities and the position opening up at Yale. He tells us how it's been his plan to come back to the United States all along, and when something opened up at Yale, it was like a dream come true.

"When did this happen?" Claudia asks.

"A month or so ago," Dad says. "That's why our plans kept changing, but I didn't want to tell any of you until it was final. The only one who knew was Grandma."

"Grandma?" I ask.

"Yes, I wanted her advice. She may not be my mother, but I really respect her." He smiles. "And I wanted to know if I could rent out the upstairs apartment until things got settled."

That makes sense. I don't know why I expected him to move back into the house and everything right away—that's just always how I pictured him here in Connecticut, I guess. But he and Mom have their own lives. It takes time for things to go back to the way they used to be, or go back to the way they're going to be, or whatever.

Maybe this is like a trial run to see if things can work out with him here. Maybe I can't totally feel like things are settled. He could leave again without warning. I just need to take it day by day.

I look at Claudia, who's smiling; and Mom, who's smiling; and Bean, who's smiling too.

"This calls for celebration!" I yell. "Ice cream sundaes, here we come!"

We all pile into the car. Bean, Claudia, and I sit in the backseat, and Dad drives. He even remembers how to get there. He remembers how to get everywhere around here. It's like he was meant to come back. He was always meant to come back.

The next week is a total whirlwind. I barely have time to just "be Lucy" like Sunny said because I barely have time to even see Yamir. We text back and forth a little bit, which is good and helps me not to overthink anything. He says he's planning to be at the grand opening and he's bringing Clint and Anthony, mostly because he heard that Leeoni's Pizza is having a table at Boat Fest right down the street from us, and it's their favorite.

I tell him Leeoni's is donating pizza for the grand opening and ribbon cutting and he texts me back that now he really has a reason to come.

I try not to get offended. Boys are just weird sometimes. I need to remind myself of that every day. Or maybe every hour.

Anais is busy every day doing final training for all the staff. She goes over how to talk to the guests, how to handle payment, tips, and greeting people in the reception area. Grandma and Mom have lunches with them too, officially welcoming them to the staff, and telling them the basics of how things work around here.

It's amazing that we now have nine new employees—four girls who do manicures, pedicures, massages, and hair blowouts and updos; three who do facials, makeup, and waxing; one who's our receptionist; and a guy who does all the upkeep, cleaning, stocking of towels, and stuff like that.

We are a fully operational spa!

I don't know if Anais said something to the staff, but they're all super-nice to me. Mara, who's one of the makeup artists, even invited me in early to show me a new shipment of makeup.

"You'll never believe the foundation," she tells me. "It's barely foundation. It's this liquid powder that goes on so smooth. Here. Sit down. I'll try it on you—not like you need it."

I hop up in our beautiful new makeup chair and Mara starts dabbing some on with one of those awesome triangular sponges. "I was so happy when I heard that the Earth Beauty line expanded into a whole new area of spa products—lotions, wax, toner. When I talked to Anais about the products you wanted to use, it was the only answer, and now we can have everything from one brand," Mara says as she's massaging in the foundation. I feel so relaxed.

"Yeah, it's the best makeup ever, and the fact that it's eco-friendly is like the icing on the cake," I say. "But now they have that higher-end line. Pure Magic. Is that what this is from?"

"Yup!" Mara hands me the mirror. "Take a look."

"Wow. So even. So smooth." I laugh. "I sound like a commercial."

Mara tells me all about her experience working at the high-end spas in Manhattan, and then wanting to move to a calmer, quieter place to raise her children. She has five-year-old twins. "It's so great here. Great schools, wonderful restaurants, a really nice tight-knit community."

"I know." I smile. "It's a great place to grow up."

After a few more hours at the spa, we all head home to rest and get ready for the big day tomorrow. It feels so weird to think that. *Tomorrow. Pink & Green is opening tomorrow.*

"I made a spaghetti feast," Bean tells all of us as we're relaxing on the deck by the pool. "I'm basically treating this grand opening weekend like a marathon, so we're doing a little carb-loading."

"Great. Just what I need." Grandma makes a face, then smiles at Bean. "I'm kidding. Thank you."

Bean finishes cooking and setting the table and tells us to be inside in about five minutes. It's going to be sad when

Bean and Claudia leave to go back to college, partly because Bean has been our cook this whole summer. He even does all the dishes. How are we ever going to go back to cooking and cleaning up for ourselves?

We all go inside and eat our spaghetti Bolognese and garlic bread and Caesar salad. Mom and Grandma have glasses of red wine. Claudia, Bean, and I have about a million glasses of Mom's mint iced tea. None of us will be able to sleep tonight. Dad had to go to Yale for the past few days to meet with some new colleagues, fill out forms, and sit in on some summer classes. But he'll be here tomorrow for the grand opening! And for the next few days while Bevin and Gary are still in the upstairs apartment, Dad's staying in our guest room.

After dinner, I call Sunny because she made me promise to call so that she could wish me good luck. Of course she'll be at the store bright and early tomorrow, but just in case I was busy, she wanted to wish me good luck in advance.

"So? You're ready?" she asks.

"I think so. I'm not the one doing all the hair and makeup for Sarabeth and her bridesmaids and moms and grandmas."

"You know what I mean, Luce." Sunny snorts. "So anyway, we'll all be there for the ribbon cutting—me, my parents, Evan, Yamir, I think Clint and Anthony too."

"Great." I'm hearing everything Sunny's saying, but I'm having trouble concentrating. I'm double-checking the spa e-mail, and my personal e-mail, and picking out different potential outfits for tomorrow.

"OK, so this is it. Tomorrow Pink and Green will be open. Everything you dreamed of will have come true!" Sunny yells into the phone.

"So amazing." I think about that, and I guess she's right. Even my dad's back, for now at least. It's hard to imagine what my life will be like without anything to worry about. Not that I'll know what that's like—there's still one big thing I have to figure out. And besides, new worries come around all the time. I used to be worried all the time about the pharmacy closing and having to sell the house, and then I was worried about my role in the spa this summer. Worrying is just a part of life.

"OK, g'night Luce. See you in the A.M.!"

"Night, Sunny."

I spend the next hour finding the perfect outfit: my frayed jean skirt and my gray ribbed tank top with my strappy black patent-leather sandals. Cute, comfy, sophisticated.

I hate to wash off the beautiful Pure Magic foundation that Mara applied before, but it's practically a law that you can't go to sleep with makeup on your face. I take one of the Earth Beauty makeup remover cloths and wipe away the foundation. It smells clean and it feels relaxing.

I go to sleep mostly free of worry, and filled with excitement and anticipation about tomorrow.

Lucy's tip for a great summer:

Wear vibrant colors and paint your toenails bright red.

Welcome! Welcome!" Mayor Danes is yelling into a megaphone. "You're all going to need to get close to your neighbors if you want to see the ribbon cutting. There are a lot of you here, and though the sidewalks on Ocean Street are wide, they're not quite wide enough for this crowd!"

I'm tempted to cover my ears because I'm so close to the megaphone and the volume is so high and Mayor Danes is yelling. But I don't. In a way, I like how loud it is. It feels big and important.

Amelia from Mayor Danes's office made a huge blowup of the press release and had it laminated and mounted on a stand outside the store. Every few seconds, someone else comes up to read the interview, and it feels pretty crazy that all of these people are reading about me.

The crowd stretches all the way down the sidewalk to Leeoni's Pizza and the Ocean View Diner and Millie's Antiques. And it stretches all the way down the other direction past the Red Cross office and the Old Mill Community Bank.

It feels a little like the ground breaking back in June, but bigger and more exciting. And Dad's here. He's standing right next to me, and he squeezes my hand, and whispers, "You did this!"

I smile. I did this. But others helped too—Morrie with the idea about Gary being an investor, and Gary finding Anais, and everything Mom put into the branding and the publicity, and Grandma being a steady force behind the prescription counter, realistic but encouraging.

"Are you ready to do the honors?" Mayor Danes turns his face toward me and away from the megaphone.

"Yes, but I want some people to help me." I look all around, then motion to Claudia and Bean to come up; we discussed it in advance that they'd help, but I didn't mention my other plan.

"Bevin?" I call. She's standing with her dad wearing some of the clothes we bought together. She looks up, confused. "Do you want to help cut the ribbon?"

Her eyes get huge and she runs up to me, and then the four of us stand there behind the big ribbon. I get to hold the scissors, and my hand is shaking a little bit. Finally I do it, and the ribbon falls to the ground and everyone starts cheering.

It's ten in the morning on a beautiful Saturday in August, and all of these people are so happy for us. Sarabeth and her friends and family will be here in an hour to primp before the wedding this evening. And then tonight Palmer and Walker will be enjoying an evening at Pink & Green.

The glass doors to Pink & Green are wide open, and people are coming in for a tour and for miniature pieces of Leeoni's donated pizzas. There's also mini spanakopita from Grecian Islands Restaurant around the corner and tea sandwiches from Max's Café three blocks down. There are avocado rolls from Gari to keep with the green theme, and pink lemonade and strawberry milk shakes from 384 Sprinkles for the pink.

People are walking around, enjoying their food, talking to each other. Soon they'll leave the spa and enjoy the rest of Boat Fest and the other booths and events.

I'm sipping a glass of pink lemonade in the Relaxation Room and taking a moment of quiet for myself, just to sit back and appreciate everything, when I feel a tap on my shoulder. I look to each side of me, and then turn around and look behind the couch.

It's Yamir.

"Hey, Luce-Juice."

"Hey."

I expect him to come and sit down with me, but he stays standing there, leaning over the top of the couch.

"So," he says.

"So."

"So now that Pink and Green is open, are you going to go back and be normal, fun Lucy again?"

"What's that supposed to mean?" I laugh.

"You know what I mean."

"Yamir, come sit, because it's really uncomfortable to keep turning my head this way to talk to you."

He gives me a crooked smile and comes to sit down.

I'm glad I asked him to sit, because my neck was starting to hurt, but now we're sitting on the couch together, alone in the Relaxation Room, and maybe it's the sourness of the lemonade, but my stomach feels like a washing machine.

"So if you go back to being normal Lucy again—"

"Wait. You're saying I used to be normal?"

He hits me on the arm. "You know what I mean."

He says that a lot. But I *do* kind of know what he means.

"If you go back to being Lucy again, and you have time for me, well, maybe we can be something . . . we can be, um, I don't know." He pauses and looks at me, and I think I know what he's getting at, but I don't know if I should say anything. "We can be . . . Lucy and Yamir."

I exhale and smile.

"I like that." I nod. "Lucy and Yamir."

"Good." He smiles, but not his crooked smile—his even, confident, self-assured smile.

"So I've only had about seventeen mini-slices of Leeoni's, which equals about one and a half real slices. Can we go get more?"

"Sure," I say.

We stand up, and as we're leaving the Relaxation Room, he grabs my hand.

We walk out through the pharmacy, still holding hands, and over to the entryway to Pink & Green.

There are people all around us—happy people, enjoying their time here. They're smiling and waving to me, and I smile back. Pink & Green sounded so great when it was just an idea I had a long time ago. Now it really exists, and it's better than I could have imagined. But right now I can only think about one thing: Lucy and Yamir.

I really like the sound of that.

Acknowledgments

Hugs, kisses, and oodles of thanks to:
Mom, Dad, Bubbie, Zeyda, Aunt Emily, Heidi, all the Rosenbergs near and far, the crew in Indiana, Libby Isaac, the BWL Library team, and everyone who has chosen to read my books.

To Ellie and Gracie, thanks for being such awesome fans! I can't wait to buy your books one day.

High fives and X's and O's for Jenny, Caroline, and Siobhan.

Alyssa, you continue to amaze me with your brilliance, honesty, sensitivity, and all-around awesomeness. If literary agenting was an Olympic sport, you would win gold every time.

Howard, Susan, Jason, Chad, Meagan, Mary Ann, Laura, Elisa, and everyone at Abrams, you are superstars. I am beyond grateful for everything that you do.

Maggie, I feel lucky every single day that you're on my team, reading my words and making each sentence better. I owe you a swimming pool of thanks.

Dave and Aleah, thanks for the love and support and for sharing vanilla milkshakes with me.

About the Author

Lisa Greenwald works in the library at the Birch Wathen Lenox School on the Upper East Side of Manhattan. She is a graduate of the New School's MFA program in writing for children. She lives with her husband and daughter in Brooklyn, New York.

This book was designed by Chad W. Beckerman. The text is set in 12-point Adobe Garamond, a typeface based on those created in the sixteenth century by Claude Garamond. Garamond modeled his typefaces on ones created by Venetian printers at the end of the fifteenth century. The modern version used in this book was designed by Robert Slimbach, who studied Garamond's historic typefaces at the Plantin-Moretus Museum in Antwerp, Belgium. The display type is Hairspray.